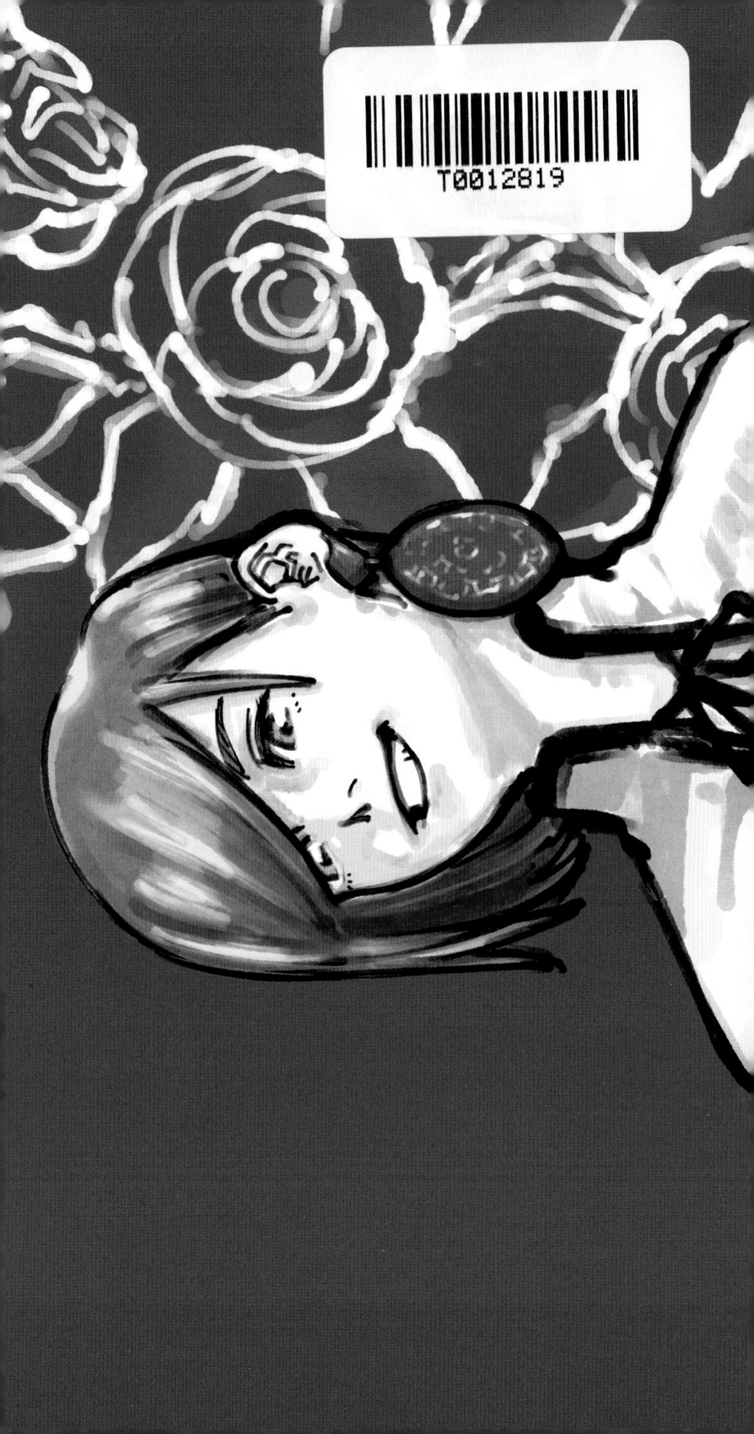

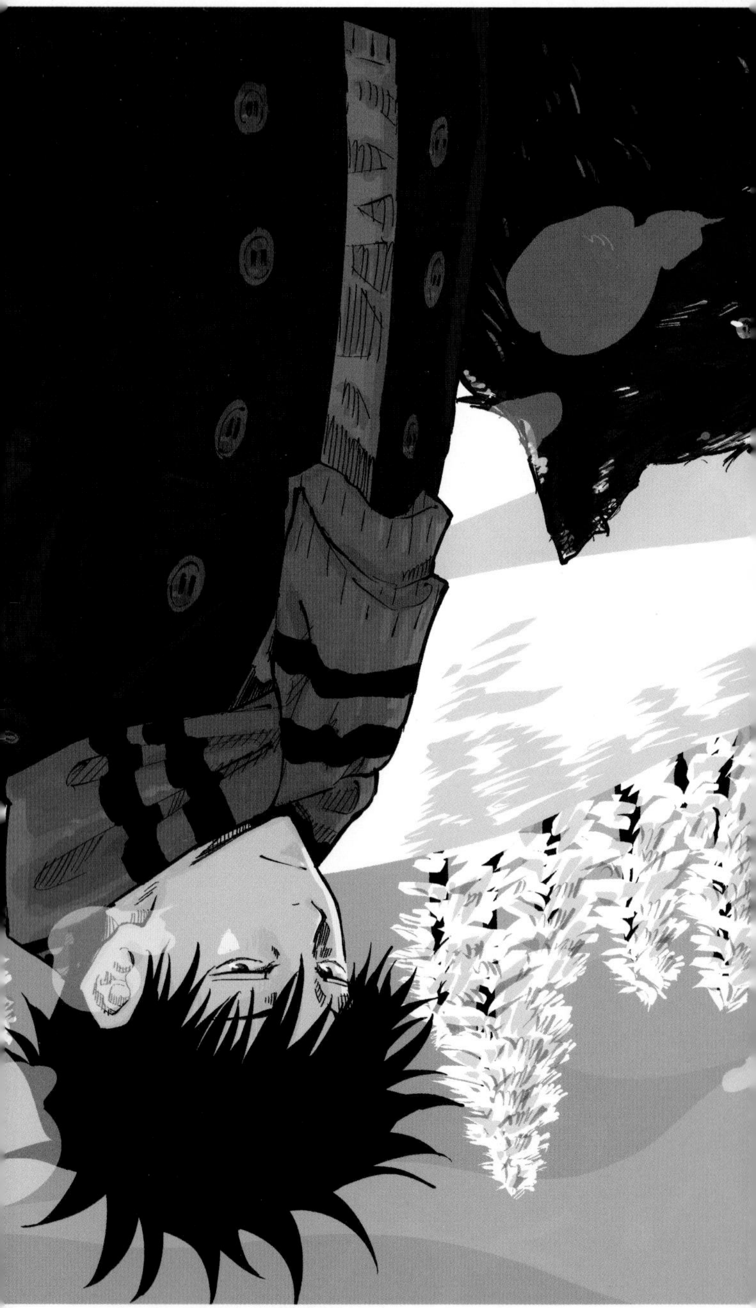

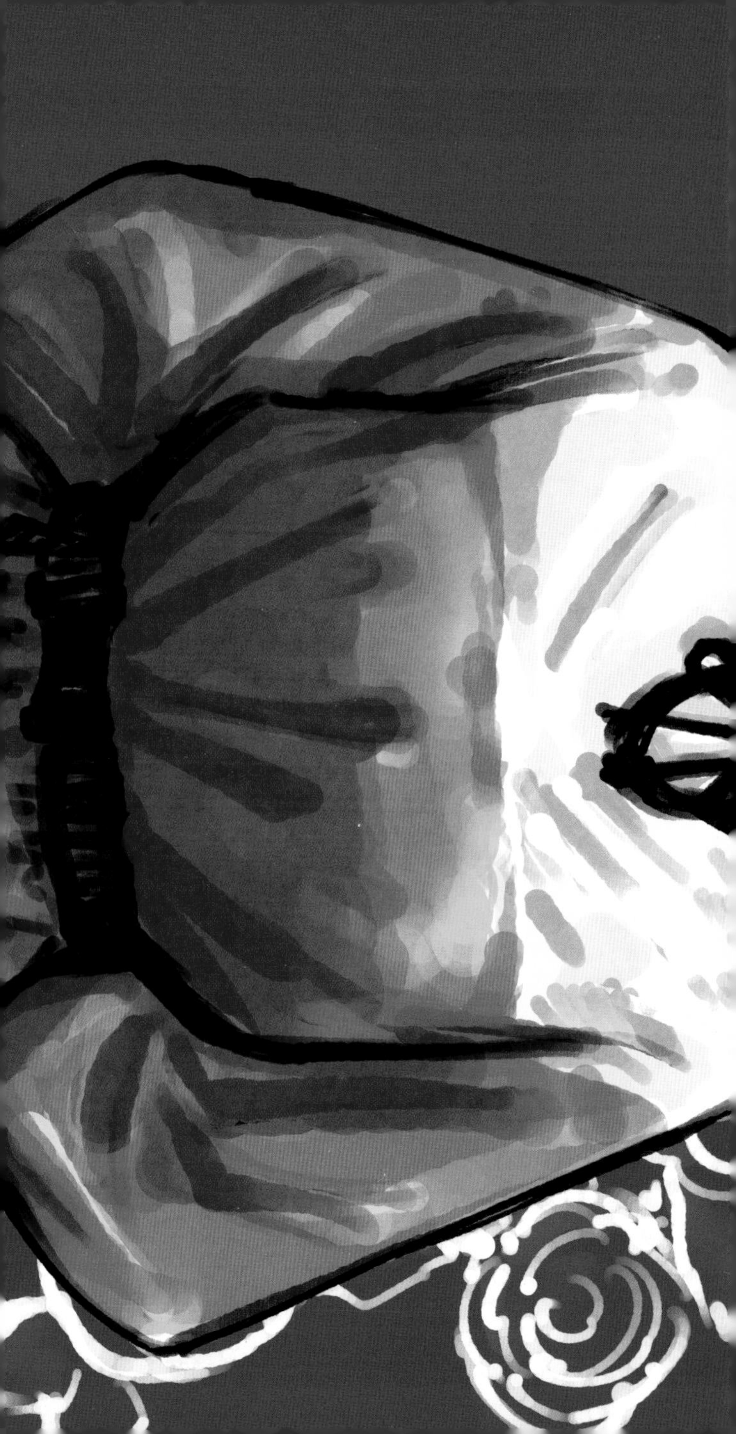

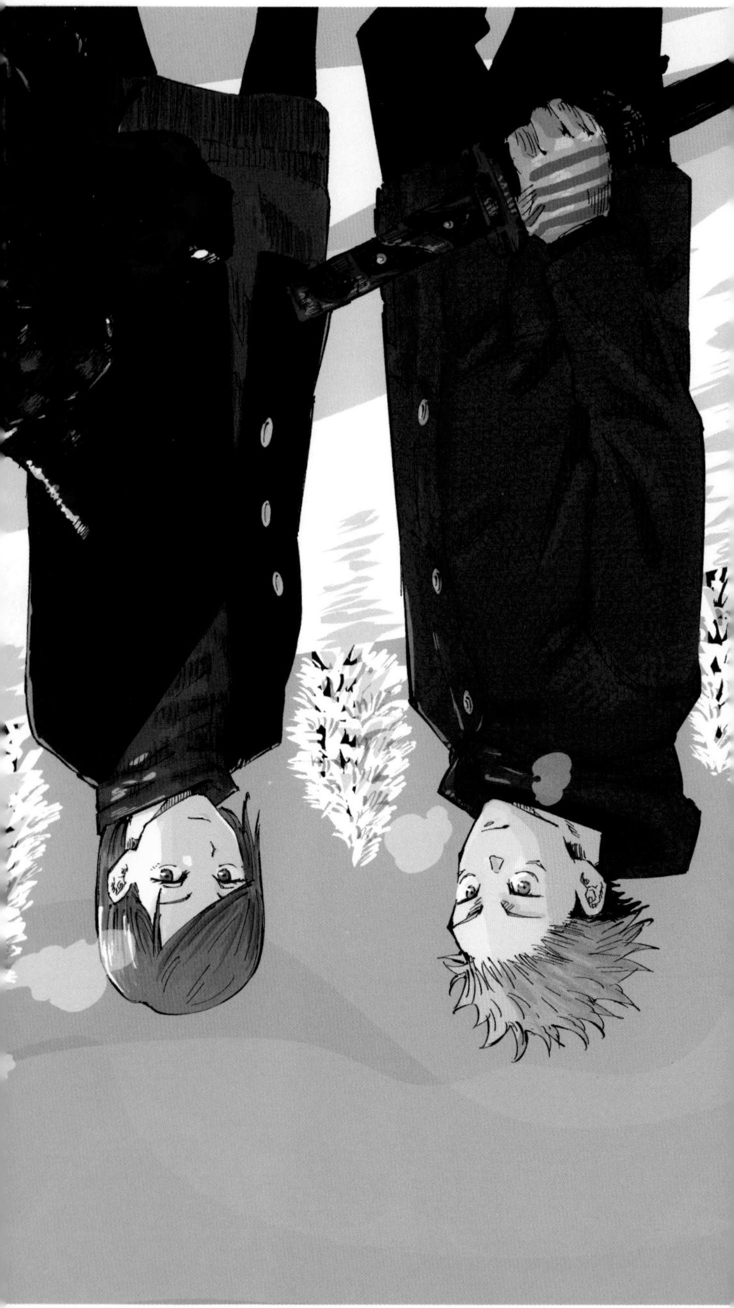

JUJUTSU KAISEN

Thorny Road at Dawn

CREATED BY
GEGE AKUTAMI

NOVEL BY
BALLAD KITAGUNI

Jujutsu High
Second-Year

Toge Inumak

Jujutsu High
Second-Year

Ultimate Mechamaru

Jujutsu Hi
Second-Ye

Mai Zen'in

Jujutsu High
Assistant Manager

Kiyotaka Ijichi

JUJUTSU KAISEN

CAST of CHARACTERS

Jujutsu High First-Year

Yuji Itadori

Jujutsu High First-Year

Megumi Fushiguro

Jujutsu High First-Year

Nobara Kugisaki

GEGE AKUTAMI

Born in 1992 in Iwate Prefecture. In 1999, Akutami was a champion in a death game that involved taking turns rubbing medication used for treating insect bites on one's nether regions, for which he attracted a lot of attention and had to disappear for a while. In 2014, Akutami began his manga career with *Kamishiro Sosa* (God Age Investigation). He claims to have no memory of that time.

At present, in 2020, *Jujutsu Kaisen* is being serialized in *Weekly Shonen Jump*. People say it's one of the "three great works inspiring déjà vu in Japan."

BALLAD KITAGUNI

Born in 19×× in Hokkaido. In 2002, Kitaguni was playing *Rurouni Kenshin* in the park with a wooden sword he'd gotten from theater class, when he got branded a suspicious individual by concerned citizens and had to disappear for a while. In 2015, Kitaguni made his authorial debut with *Apricot Red*. Kitaguni hides this information from his relatives.

At present, in 2020, Kitaguni is supposed to be working on a novelization but is distracted by the idea of someone rubbing medication for insect bites on their nether regions in a death game...

JUJUTSU KAISEN

Thorny Road at Dawn

JUJUTSU KAISEN
Thorny Road at Dawn

JUJUTSU KAISEN YOAKE NO IBARAMICHI
© 2020 by Gege Akutami, Ballad Kitaguni
All rights reserved.
First published in Japan in 2020 by SHUEISHA Inc., Tokyo.
English translation rights arranged by SHUEISHA Inc.

COVER AND INTERIOR DESIGN Shawn Carrico
TRANSLATION John Werry
EDITOR Megan Bates

Published by VIZ Media, LLC
P.O. Box 77010
San Francisco, CA 94107

Library of Congress Cataloging-in-Publication Data

Names: Kitaguni, Ballad, author. | Werry, John (Translator), translator. |
Akutami, Gege, 1992- creator.
Title: Jujutsu Kaisen, thorny road at dawn / created by Gege Akutami ; novel
by Baraddo Kitaguni ; translated by John Werry.
Other titles: Jujutsu Kaisen yoake no ibaramichi. English
Description: San Francisco : Viz Media, 2023. | Series: Jujutsu Kaisen |
Summary: A modeling scout approaches Kugisaki, but he turns out to be a
cursed speech user with an ulterior motive, while Mechamaru goes on a
solo mission, Gojo and friends try to host a party, and more adventures
ensue in five short stories set in the world of Jujutsu Kaisen.
Identifiers: LCCN 2022040019 (print) | LCCN 2022040020 (ebook) | ISBN
9781974732562 (paperback) | ISBN 9781974738472 (ebook)
Subjects: CYAC: Fantasy. | Supernatural--Fiction. | Demonology--Fiction. |
Magic--Fiction. | LCGFT: Paranormal fiction. | Action and adventure
fiction. | Short stories. | Light novels.
Classification: LCC PZ7.1.K627 Juj 2023 (print) | LCC PZ7.1.K627 (ebook)
| DDC [Fic]--dc23
LC record available at https://lccn.loc.gov/2022040019
LC ebook record available at https://lccn.loc.gov/2022040020

Printed in the U.S.A.
First Printing, April 2023

viz.com

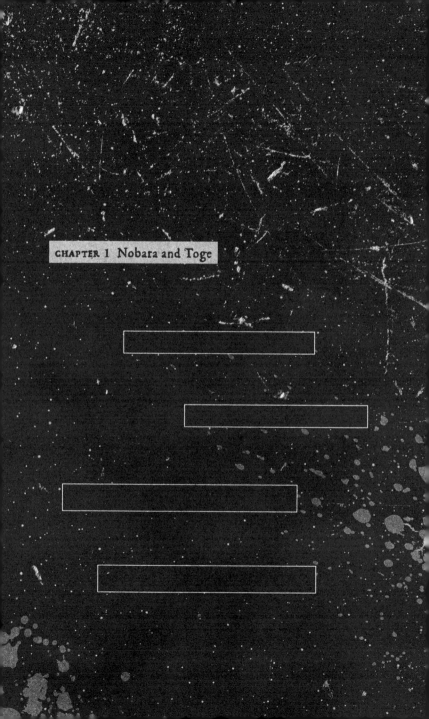

CHAPTER 1 Nobara and Toge

"Toge?" Panda tilted his head as he spoke to Kugisaki.

It was the beginning of August. She was in the midst of rebounding off a tree in the Tokyo Prefectural Jujutsu High School courtyard at a 180-degree angle. This was during grueling first-year training as the school geared up for the upcoming Goodwill Event with their sister school in Kyoto. The focus was hand-to-hand combat, specifically battles between jujutsu sorcerers.

Or rather, it was *supposed* to be a training session, but not much was happening other than Kugisaki repeatedly rushing Panda, who kept sending her flying back, only to have her rush at him again, over and over. Todo and Mai's role was to encourage her, and she did indeed appear motivated, so perhaps their efforts were having an effect.

"Yes. I can tell Maki respects him, and you say he's a skilled sorcerer, Panda Senpai," Kugisaki replied.

"You don't use the senpai honorific for Maki, who's also in a higher grade than you. You don't have to use it for me either," Panda said.

"I respect you," Kugisaki said as she stood up again, brushing tree leaves off her tracksuit. "Besides, calling you Panda would feel sorta whimsical."

"Well, your ability to engage in chitchat while getting knocked around is impressive, at least," Panda said.

"Getting a thrashing like this will teach me defense," Kugisaki said.

Panda looked around and confirmed that Toge, who had gone to the drugstore, hadn't returned yet. He managed to do this while also defending against Kugisaki, who had rushed him again. He easily deflected her and continued speaking. "Anyway, what about Toge?"

"I'm wondering what he's like as a senpai," Kugisaki replied.

"Hm? Can't you tell by talking to him?"

"Of course not! I mean, I know he's not a bad guy, but I can't tell much more since his vocabulary consists solely of rice-ball ingredients."

"I guess we've gotten used to it," Panda said. "Right, Maki?"

"Yeah," Maki answered. "But I suppose I can understand her confusion."

Maki spun a pole-like cursed tool, nimbly dodged an attack by Fushiguro, and—*bonk!*—scored a light hit on Fushiguro's head.

"Ow!" Fushiguro exclaimed in pain.

"You still think too much with your head," Maki chided. She gave him a disdainful glance. She didn't seem to be out of breath at all, looking even more at ease than Panda. "Toge's probably the most considerate of us all," she said.

"Despite his first impression, he's a smart guy. Aside from Yuta, he's the best in our grade," Panda added.

"His only flaw is that he can be pretty mischievous," said Maki.

Panda said, "He's not *that* mischievous, is he?"

"You don't notice it because you're mischievous *with* him!"

"That hurts. We aren't mischievous. We're just spirited."

Kugisaki had reached the limit of her ability to make small talk while training. The second-years continued conversing about trivialities, operating on a completely different level than her. But the moment Panda diverted his attention ever so slightly toward his conversation with Maki, Kugisaki feinted left and then right and threw an uppercut.

"Anyway..." Panda easily swayed aside to evade the attack, then tripped Kugisaki with a sobat-like move.

"*Geh!*" she cried out.

The leg Kugisaki was using to pivot collapsed. She spun and fell, but without letting down her guard. It was a reflex she'd been honing over the past few weeks. However, defending isn't the same as winning, and her disappointment was apparent in her expression.

"Toge's a good guy. You'll learn soon enough," Panda said, looking down at her.

"If you say so," Kugisaki responded.

Kugisaki's defense also didn't prevent her from injuring her back when she fell. *If I keep falling like this, I'll have to buy a new tracksuit*, she thought dejectedly.

Sometime later, on an autumn day during a short school break following the incident at Yasohachi Bridge, Kugisaki decided to go to Shibuya alone.

Fushiguro was exhausted and had holed up in his room to read, while Itadori had gone out to see an arty movie that only a film nerd would like. Maki was on a mission unrelated to the Yasohachi Bridge incident, so they wouldn't see each other for a while. This left Kugisaki without any plans, so she went shopping for makeup, clothes and personal items—things she wouldn't want to shop for with the boys around.

"Winter tops and bottoms, winter shoes, underwear, foundation," she muttered to herself.

With shopping bags dangling from both hands, Kugisaki examined her haul. She didn't think she'd purchased too much, but she had done more walking than expected. Perhaps it had been a mistake to wear her new pin-heeled boots. She didn't get to go shopping alone that often, though, and there were still some things she wanted to look for. As she walked through the boisterous crowd, she thought she might browse handbags next.

When she had first arrived in Tokyo, all the new sights were dazzling to her. Three months later, she had grown accustomed to the lights, and the noise had even started to get on her nerves. But it was a product of unceasing human activity, and the constant snippets of conversation gave the city character.

"That was a masterpiece!"

"Salmon!"

"Come visit our new shop! We reopened!"

"Don't you want to try some? It's delicious!"

"Did we get too much?"

"I'm so tired!"

"Mom, buy that for me!"

Countless voices representing countless lives intermingled at the intersection. Each one was an individual, existing in their own individual world. Some people might've found the confusion of voices and needs to be depressing, but not Kugisaki. She had a strong sense of self. She welcomed the clamor of the city, because it allowed everyone to live as they pleased.

Actually, it was her home village that had been suffocating. There, conformity was encouraged. Its ecosystem survived by refusing to recognize individuals as individuals. To Kugisaki, it had felt like a closed-off world that was quietly rotting away. By contrast, the masses of people in the city meant that every person had their freedom. Someone once said that the city makes you lose interest in other people. Kugisaki smiled, thinking that was fine by her. No one here would criticize her for being who she was, and she could walk wherever her own two feet took her. The chaotic and multifaceted nature of the city was comfortable for her.

Yet fateful encounters occur even in the urban jumble.

"Hmm?"

Kugisaki was walking toward Shibuya Hikarie when she recognized a face amidst the crowd on the other side of the street. The person's collar was flipped up and closed tight, hiding the lower half of his face. It was Toge Inumaki. She was certain she had never met the blue-eyed man with him, who looked as though he might be a foreign tourist. The unexpected sight of the two captured Kugisaki's interest.

"I wonder what they're talking about."

Kugisaki changed her trajectory, crossed the street just as the signal changed, and made for Inumaki. As she approached, she could overhear his conversation.

"I'd like to go to Shibuya 109," the man with blue eyes said.

"Salmon, salmon," Inumaki replied.

"Where can I get a taxi?" asked the man.

"Salted fish roe."

"Um...which way should we go?"

"Kelp."

"Uh...*watashi...ikitai. Ichimaru Kyū,*" the man stammered in Japanese. "Please, okay?"

"Salmon," Toge responded

"Salmon?" the man repeated.

"Salm...on."

"Salmon again?! What the heck, man?!"

"Fish flakes."

"Ugh..."

This situation was even more of a disaster than Kugisaki could have imagined. Inumaki was a cursed speech user, so in order to avoid accidentally releasing curses, the only words he uttered were rice ball ingredients. This tourist had stopped *him*, of all people, to ask for directions, and Inumaki was trying to respond the best he could through a variety of gestures.

Figuring the tourist was probably running out of patience, Kugisaki decided to intervene. "What's up, Senpai?"

"Tuna mayo," Inumaki answered.

"Spare me the rice-ball bit, okay?"

"Ooh, a geisha girl!" said the tourist.

"Who you callin' a geisha girl?!" Kugisaki demanded.

From what she'd overheard, Kugisaki had an idea of where he wanted to go. She managed to direct him to the other side of the station with four simple English words: "Left, right, straight...goddamnit!"

Having finally received directions, the tourist stumped off, but not before expressing his appreciation with an antiquated term, saying, "*Katajikenōgozaru!*"

Inumaki's not the only weirdo around here, Kugisaki thought.

"Salmon," Inumaki said.

"Come on, couldn't you have written down directions? Or shown him a map on your phone?" Kugisaki asked.

"Salted fish roe."

Kugisaki had met Inumaki about three months ago, but she still couldn't understand rice ball-ese. Apparently, Fushiguro could, and Itadori had the ability to play along. Naturally, the second-years could understand too.

Inumaki had helped Kugisaki with her sparring, so he wasn't exactly a stranger. And during the plot to kill Itadori—of which no proof remained—Inumaki had been worried about Itadori, even though they had just met. So Kugisaki knew he wasn't a bad guy, but there were limits to how well she would be able to get to know him if all he could do was call out rice ball ingredients.

She knew that Maki respected Inumaki, and Panda, who had been Kugisaki's sparring partner, relied on him. They had both declared him a good guy. Nonetheless, Kugisaki had yet to really get a handle on her senpai Inumaki.

The problem was compatibility. Kugisaki was a talker who tended to let her words spill out. She found it hard to deal with Inumaki, who only responded with rice-ball ingredients.

She didn't particularly want to be brusque with close acquaintances, but the straightforward way relatives and close acquaintances speak to each other affirms the kind of trust that doesn't require formalities. She had difficulty with Inumaki's type of communication, because she could never understand what he was getting at.

That didn't mean that she disliked him. And she didn't want to be rough with him. As a result, she was taking extra care with her words, and that irritated her. Words were an expression of the soul, so she didn't want them to be distorted. She found this whole balancing act to be uncomfortable. *Excruciating*, in fact.

"Whatever," she said. "But the next time someone annoying talks to you, just ignore it. Now I've got shopping to do. See ya."

"Mustard leaf," her senpai replied.

"Yeah, yeah. 'Mustard leaf' to you too!"

Kugisaki had no idea what that meant, but Inumaki had said it as they parted, so it seemed natural to say it back. As she took a step away, Inumaki grabbed her shoulder and stopped her.

"Uh...whaddaya need?" she asked.

"Fish flakes."

"Sorry, that doesn't tell me much."

Inumaki waved his hands and shook his head. Kugisaki got the sense that he didn't want her to keep shopping, but she couldn't figure out why that would be. Maybe he just wanted her to head back before it got dark. In any case, that was all she was picking up, because "fish flakes" just didn't provide detail.

She knew he was worried, though, so she smiled. "Don't worry. I won't stay out too late wandering around."

"Mustard leaf," he said.

"Uh-huh. Don't you stay out too late either," Kugisaki said, casting a vexed look at him before rejoining the crowd.

"Fish flakes!"

Inumaki reached out again, but his hand banged into an old lady who was passing by. Thankfully, he didn't hurt her, but as he was helping her across the street, Kugisaki moved out of sight.

Nobara and Toge

Kugisaki passed a building and turned a corner. She strolled through the waves of people coming and going, and she was good at dodging criers as they handed out flyers and tissue packets. As she blew past, she thought, *Good job, guys!*

"H-h-hold on, Miss!" someone called out. "Pardon me, but have you got a sec?"

"Hunh?!" Kugisaki exclaimed.

A pushy man was shoving his way toward her. He planted himself right in front of her, blocking her from going any further. He had long blond hair and a goatee, and he was wearing a suit. He was slender and had such a dark tan that his white teeth dazzled when he smiled.

"So?" Kugisaki demanded. "Let me guess, you want me to model for you. Well, I've already had enough offers."

"Aw, don't be cold," the man replied. "Lemme introduce myself."

He held out a business card, and Kugisaki took it with her right hand, shopping bags dangling from her wrist. The cultural conditioning to accept a business card when someone offers it is strong.

"Just like it says there, I'm Kaya Tsurube from H Productions, a fashion-model agency."

"H Productions... It really *is* a modeling agency?"

Kugisaki peered at the business card, then at the man named Tsurube, then at the card once more.

"Huh?" she said. "Seriously? You're a *scout*?"

"Sure, if you wanna call it that. Sorry to be so pushy, but the modeling world is cutthroat when it comes to recruiting. I gotta bother any diamond in the rough that I spot shining brighter than everyone else. The way *you* do!"

H Production... Modeling... Diamond in the rough...

As if those dreamlike words weren't enough, Tsurube piled on more. "My agency's new motto for the next generation is 'cute and powerful,' and you fit that description perfectly!"

"Well...yeah!" Kugisaki responded. "You've got a good eye!"

"So if you don't mind, I wanna talk for a minute," Tsurube continued. "You really are a diamond in the rough. You must be busy, but one conversation could change your future, so I think it's worth your time. I have a feeling you could be the next Jennifer Lawrence!"

"Really?" Kugisaki was intrigued. "In that case, I'll at least listen."

"I knew it! I knew you wouldn't pass up this opportunity!"

He really lays it on thick, Kugisaki thought. It felt good, however, to be complimented by an industry professional. She'd imagined just this scenario many times as she walked around the city. Maybe this was really happening!

"But you're carrying stuff, so we shouldn't talk in the street like this," Tsurube said. "Come with me somewhere nice and quiet where we can talk."

Tsurube gave Kugisaki a nudge and she began walking, somewhat dreamily.

"An H Pro model…" She liked the sound of that. Practically speaking, it wouldn't be possible to be both a sorcerer and a model, but it would be a shame to turn down this opportunity without enjoying it a little first. At the very least, it would make a good story. Although it wasn't like her, she found herself thinking, *Yeah, I believe this guy!*

Shaking off these strange thoughts, Kugisaki walked down an alley Tsurube had steered her toward. In that moment, she had no reason to suspect that she wasn't walking of her own volition.

Kugisaki came to herself, but only partially, over ten minutes later. What called her back were the bonds cinching her hands behind her back. That was when she finally realized how weird the whole sequence of events had been.

She was sitting in a room that didn't look at all like it belonged to an entertainment agency, containing just one simple desk and a bookshelf, other than the chair she was tied to. Seals with occult symbols covered every inch of the walls and even the floor. At a glance, she knew that someone involved with jujutsu had prepared this space.

"What's the big idea, you slimeball?!" she exclaimed.

"Oh, you're awake?" Tsurube replied. "Go easy on the insults, yeah?"

He was sitting behind a desk cutting a cigar with a knife. He looked at Kugisaki, then flicked his gaze behind her and said, "I told you to be gentle, Koizumi! You were too rough. It jolted her back to herself!"

"S-sorry, Tsurube!" said the man—Koizumi, apparently—who was standing behind her. "But she had a hammer! It scared me!"

Koizumi was a wall of muscle. He looked larger than Todo. His professional wrestler's build didn't at all match his timid demeanor.

"Well, the rope is just a safety measure, and I hafta say I'm surprised at how easily she woke up anyway," Tsurube said. "Kugisaki—that's your name, right? You must have a strong sense of self. I'm surprised."

"Hunh?" Kugisaki responded.

The veins in her temples bulged as she realized how *not* good her situation was. They had slung her over the back of the chair, arms draped over the backrest. And from the way her sleeves felt, they had probably taken her hammer, nails, and doll.

"How do you know my name?" she demanded.

"You told me yourself, but I doubt you'd remember," Tsurube answered. He lowered his head, looking down at her across the desk. The glare from the setting sun was shining through the window and making his expression hard to see, but it looked like he was smirking. "Take it easy, Kugisaki. We don't plan on hurtin' ya. We just wanna talk."

"Hunh? Why would I believe—"

"Just *believe* me, yeah?"

Kugisaki wanted to shout at him then, but her anger disappeared as soon as it formed. It felt so easy to just believe what he said, as Tsurube had suggested, and part of her longed to *take it easy*. The rational part of her realized how weird this was, but she found that she couldn't doubt him, no matter how much she wanted to put up her mental defenses. She had fallen into a state that was incomprehensible even to herself.

Still, she could summon at least a measure of fighting spirit.

"Stop smirking," she said.

Kugisaki realized they hadn't tied her legs, so she shot to her feet. The rope tying her to the chair tightened painfully. She twisted her body and swung the legs of the chair at Tsurube.

"N-not gonna happen," Koizumi said.

She had made solid contact, but the only result was that the chair broke. The big man had stepped between her and Tsurube. She had swung with all her might, but he showed no sign of having suffered the slightest injury.

"*Tch*," Kugisaki huffed.

Kugisaki was much smaller than Koizumi, so she was the one who had ended up on the floor. She immediately tried to stand up, but the chair interfered and she remained on her side, floundering.

"Don't bother, Kugisaki. When it comes to sheer brute force, Koizumi is first-rate. He's a total doofus about complicated cursed techniques, but his physical strength plus a cursed technique for re inforcing skin with cursed energy turn him into the ultimate shield."

"Then I'll bust *your* head first," Kugisaki threatened.

"I'm so scared," Tsurube replied. "But I wouldn't count on it."

Those words alone were enough to wither Kugisaki's desire to resist. Although her eyes still simmered with spite, she could no longer entertain thoughts of defeating her captors.

Chuckling, Tsurube waved his finger and said, "Listen. My cursed technique is cursed speech."

"Cursed speech?" Kugisaki repeated.

She thought of Inumaki. Even she knew that cursed speech was dangerous. If she had to defend herself against the one-two punch of Koizumi's immense strength and Tsurube's cursed speech, the situation was dire indeed.

"Yes." Tsurube answered. "But my people ain't like the vaunted Inumaki family. We ain't as strong or versatile. Even with an amplifier, we barely compare, so don't worry."

"Amplifier?" Kugisaki asked.

"I gave you my card, right? It's made from an ancient cursed tree called *tsurube-oroshi*. It's connected to the cursed seal on my tongue. Likewise, the wallpaper covering every bit of this room consists of seals made from a single tree. It all functions as my tongue. I put a ton of effort into its construction. It's a barrier almost exactly like a domain. As for my cursed speech..."

That was when Kugisaki, whose thoughts had been fuzzy, realized that the danger was mounting, because Tsurube was disclosing his cursed technique. Even worse, he was disclosing his cursed technique as a *cursed speech user*. Kugisaki's warrior instincts were on high alert— she knew she shouldn't listen, but she couldn't move her hands to plug her ears.

As Kugisaki's alarm increased, Tsurube uttered the key words: "My cursed speech is inconvenient but simple. You simply *have* to believe what I say."

Now Kugisaki realized the situation was as bad as it could be. Tsurube's cursed speech merely gave words credibility. However, combining that with the disclosure of his cursed technique had a synergistic effect. The Binding Vow required him to reveal his ability as interlocked with his cursed speech, thereby *compelling* belief, and that was powerful.

Kugisaki was compelled to believe even his explanation of her compulsion to believe; what's more, the seals that covered the room amplified that effect. Layer upon layer put her at a disadvantage. How much had he made her believe before she woke up? What suggestions had he given her? She had no way of knowing.

"Don't worry," Tsurube said. "You just gotta listen like a good girl. You do that, and I won't hurt ya."

"And yet you've *tied me up*," she said.

"Seriously, you gotta believe me," Tsurube went on. "And you *do*, right? You already believe me."

Tsurube's cursed speech compelled her to believe him when he stated that she believed him. She felt like she was going crazy.

"Just chill," he said. "I ain't gonna take your life. But I want you to tell me something about Jujutsu High, where you go to school."

"How do you know I'm a high school student?" she asked.

"Well, guys like me have a network," he responded. "So I know that three new first-years just enrolled, and that there's a loser grade 3 newb, and what they all look like. We know that much. I buy the info, then get more details about Jujutsu High from small-time rookie sorcerers. It's my business."

"Oh..."

Kugisaki wondered if Tsurube and his network had connections to curse users involved with special grade cursed spirits, but decided that was unlikely. A group like that would be able to infiltrate Jujutsu High, so there would be no need to resort to such circuitous ways of gathering information. Even so, she wanted to avoid telling them anything about school: its layout, the nature of the barrier that protected it, information about staff. Jujutsu High was the locus of the sorcerers' activities, a place for developing combat strength. She didn't want to reveal even the slightest piece of information to anyone who was so clearly opposed to Jujutsu High.

Before Tsurube's cursed speech completely demolished her judgment and she told them whatever they asked, she needed to enact a countermeasure. At the very least, she needed to take action while she was still capable of formulating such thoughts. She considered that biting through her own tongue might eventually be necessary.

Or maybe I need to do that now, *before I lose all sense of myself and forget who Nobara Kugisaki is*, she thought.

Just as she was solidifying her resolve, a loud sound—*wham!*—came from outside the room.

"Hunh?" Tsurube grunted.

The sound distracted Kugisaki's opponents, presenting her with a momentary opportunity. But she couldn't even stand up; all she could do was grind her teeth.

Tsurube thought for a moment, then issued an order to Koizumi. "Was that a mouse? Go take a look," he directed. "This girl won't cause us any trouble for a while. You can handle bullets and stuff, though, so it's safer for you."

"S-sure," Koizumi agreed, creeping toward the door. He was so big that he'd have to stoop to fit through it. He turned the doorknob, bent double, and stuck out his head.

"Sleep," a voice said.

"What?"

It was the last thing Koizumi said before his massive form collapsed like a tranquilized bear or a marionette whose strings had been cut. He sprawled by the door, now looking like a giant doorstop.

Before Kugisaki could grasp what was happening, a figure jumped into the room and launched toward Tsurube. Tsurube blocked a hand chop that flew at his face but not the fist that jabbed his solar plexus an instant later. A dull sound rang out.

"Guh... *Agh*!" Tsurube cried out. His body folded and he collapsed.

Kugisaki couldn't clearly see what was happening because of her position on the floor and the glare from the setting sun, but she realized right away who had forced his way in.

"Inumaki Senpai?" she asked.

"Salmon," he replied. Then he closed his collar, hiding his mouth's cursed seal, and turned to face her. "Kelp."

"That's not very reassuring," she said.

"Salmon roe."

"Just kidding. Thanks."

"Salmon, salmon."

Inumaki used the knife Tsurube had been using on his cigar to cut Kugisaki's ropes. Her skin hurt where the rope had chafed, but she was able to struggle to her feet.

She considered asking Inumaki why he had come, but of course he wouldn't be able to explain. She decided to use her own head. She figured the reason was pretty simple: Inumaki was a semi-grade 1 sorcerer on a solo mission. When he had encountered Kugisaki walking around alone in the city, he had tried to warn her about something. Shortly thereafter, she had fallen into the enemy's hands. Inumaki had been targeting Tsurube the whole time.

Kugisaki couldn't help but wish that she had simply listened to Inumaki's warning. But how was she supposed to understand when the only words he said were rice-ball ingredients? Well, she could at least try to remember that fish flakes and mustard leaf didn't have very bright connotations.

"We gotta escape," she said. "But we should tie up those sham recruiters first."

"Salmon," Inumaki said.

"I guess 'salmon' sorta expresses agreement?" she guessed.

"Salmon," he responded.

"That's so simple...yet so hard to—Watch out!!"

"Salted fish roe?" he asked.

A large figure appeared behind him. Koizumi had woken from Inumaki's cursed speech and risen from the floor. Inumaki immediately tried to free his mouth, but Koizumi's fist was already coming down.

"Get out of the way," Kugisaki shouted.

She shot forward like a bullet, thrusting her senpai aside and heading straight for Koizumi. The goliath was already on the move, but Kugisaki was faster. Without her hammer, she couldn't use her Straw Doll technique, but that didn't mean she couldn't fight.

In fact, she was all too accustomed to fighting larger opponents. Silently thanking Panda, Kugisaki threw her full weight into an elbow jab to Koizumi's solar plexus. It worked, maybe a little *too* well.

"Huh?" Kugisaki was surprised at how easily Koizumi went down. His stomach muscles hadn't even tensed—he just fell as if he had had no intention of defending himself. Kugisaki's puzzlement quickly turned into alarm. At the sound of violent coughing, Kugisaki turned to see Tsurube. He was on his feet and glaring at her as he stepped on Inumaki, who had fallen and was clutching his throat.

"Inumaki Senpai?!" Kugisaki exclaimed.

"Damn brats wanna go causin' trouble, eh?!" Tsurube shouted.

His face no longer wore the smirk it had moments ago. His bulging eyes were full of malice. His tongue, forked like a snake's, peeked from his mouth, which bore the patterns of a cursed seal.

"Koizumi is a decoy," he explained. "I gave him a command so that even if he loses consciousness, he wakes up a given period of time later. That's how I was able to take down this meddler. I always have a backup plan."

"What did you do to Inumaki?!" Kugisaki demanded.

"The Inumaki family is well-known, and I was able to ascertain that one of their cursed speech users is at Jujutsu High," Tsurube answered. "So of *course* I took precautions."

Koizumi picked up a wet cloth that had fallen to the floor and flourished it.

Tsurube said, "It's a kind of homemade tear gas, like mace. Cursed speech users have ways of defending against each other's cursed speech. Especially a strong cursed speech user. Uttering just one word puts pressure on the throat. It's instantaneous."

"Huh?" Kugisaki said. "Inumaki wouldn't fall for that so easily!"

"I owe it to you, Kugisaki," Tsurube said. "He's your senpai, so when he saw an unknown object flying at you, he didn't hesitate to leap to your defense. He's such a *caring* guy."

Something inside Kugisaki snapped. Anger over her own carelessness made her blood boil, driving away all thought. She had just doubled the trouble she caused Inumaki.

Why did he go out on an investigation alone? It was because of compatibility with his target. For targeting a cursed speech user, another cursed speech user like Inumaki would have the most suitable knowledge. Alone, he would have been able to handle this easily, because the enemy was hardly formidable. But Tsurube and Koizumi had gotten the best of her twice, thereby exposing Inumaki to danger when he came to rescue her.

She was filled with a single emotion, which cleared away all extraneous thought and distraction. That emotion was anger. Pure anger. Not at her opponents, but at herself.

The sunset stained the room blood red. As the desk, walls, and floor turned crimson, what seemed most vivid to Kugisaki was the target she needed to hit. Her agitation hadn't disrupted her reason; instead, sheer fury had sharpened her resolve.

"Careful now," Tsurube warned. "You shouldn't raise your hand to me, Kugisaki. I already got you to tell me your cursed technique. Straw Doll, right? I have your hammer, so you can't use it. So just stop, yeah? You shouldn't even consider trying to harm—"

"Shut up," Kugisaki said.

"Huh?" Tsurube looked astonished at having been interrupted.

His cursed speech should have been binding her spirit. She shouldn't have been able to find the will to interrupt his words. He didn't think she had the mental fortitude to resist his amplified cursed speech, especially since she was weak, an inexperienced brat, and a grade 3 sorcerer.

But he didn't know. He didn't know that the girl before his eyes *wasn't* weak. More than *an inexperienced brat* or *a grade 3 sorcerer*, she was *Nobara Kugisaki*.

"I'd rather listen to someone vomiting," Kugisaki said. She took Tsurube's business card from her pocket.

She had just seen the effects of cursed speech firsthand, so now she realized the danger of this power that could cause harm with a mere word. Inumaki's sacrifice—abandoning using normal speech so that he could seal away this danger—was immense.

Why had he risked himself to protect Kugisaki from Tsurube's knock-out drug? Because he wasn't able to warn her. His mouth formed words that became reality, so he couldn't say "danger." And because of that, he hadn't hesitated to be her shield.

Inumaki spoke words and abandoned words for the benefit of others. Tsurube's glib jabbering was worthless compared to Inumaki's sparse utterances.

Kugisaki tossed Tsurube's card to the floor and raised one leg.

"Um, I wouldn't bother," Tsurube scoffed.

Then he remembered her cursed technique: *Straw Doll involves remotely infusing a doll with cursed energy.* But he had taken away her hammer and doll, so there should be no way for her to use this technique, should there? She was acting out of mere desperation. She had to be.

A small form dropped from Kugisaki's hand onto the business card. It was a doll made of the rope they had used to bind Kugisaki's hands. She had fashioned a rudimentary doll from the rope's frayed ends.

Any sorcerer whose cursed technique required a medium would understand the great danger of losing that medium. It would only make sense that such a sorcerer would acquire the skill of *creating* a medium from whatever was close at hand. Kugisaki had her doll, and as for a nail to charge with cursed energy...

Tsurube's eyes then focused on the pin heels of the boots she was wearing.

"H-hey... No, don't—" he said. He was unable to think of anything to say that would be an effective counter before she brought down her boot. *Don't* or *stop* alone wouldn't carry sufficient meaning. Tsurube's cursed speech couldn't force behavior; it could only instill belief. It wouldn't work if the words weren't substantial enough.

Even now, however, he wasn't worried. Kugisaki only intended to use Straw Doll for an attack via the business card, which was made from the same tree as the cursed seals around the room, and that was too broad a target. The damage from a cursed energy blast coming from a mere grade 3 sorcerer would be diffused to almost nothing among the countless seals.

There's no problem, Tsurube assured himself.

However, the only thing he'd gotten out of Kugisaki while she was brainwashed was the nature of her cursed technique. He had no reason to suspect she was anything but some grade 3 sorcerer, a loser newb. Kugisaki wasn't someone who could be so easily reduced to simple categories.

"It's useless, you damn brat!" he shouted. "Struggle all you want, but—"

"I told you to shut up." she interrupted him.

With one stomp of her boot, she pierced the doll and the business card. Her honed cursed energy rushed out, and all the seals went up in flames. So did Tsurube's tongue, which was linked to the seals.

"*Agh! Uaaaaaagh! Ngah! Hungh! Uwaaaaaah!*" Tsurube writhed in excruciating pain as his tongue split like a blooming flower.

Kugisaki looked down at him, then opened the desk drawer in a leisurely way and removed her hammer, nails and straw doll.

"*Aaaaaugh!*" Tsurube screamed again. He was staggering toward the door, looking as if he might collapse at any moment. As intense as the pain assailing him was, he could still sense the danger to his life and knew he had to escape.

He seemed a sorry sight, but Kugisaki couldn't allow him to leave. She didn't know how much information she had revealed while under the influence of his cursed speech, and thought it was probably best to put an end to him right now.

She tossed a nail into the air and swung her hammer, but a split second before she struck it, she heard a hoarse command.

"Don't...kill...him," Inumaki stammered.

"*Yaaiieeeeee!*" Tsurube screamed.

The distraction had caused Kugisaki to divert the nail to Tsurube's ankle, which prevented him from moving. If he couldn't flee, that was enough. Kugisaki checked to make sure he was immobile, then dropped her gaze to Inumaki, who was still on the floor, clutching his throat.

"...fish flakes..." he said.

"Aw, come on," she replied.

Inumaki was back to only naming rice-ball ingredients, but Kugisaki understood what had transpired. He hadn't forced those words of normal speech through his damaged throat out of concern for Tsurube; he had done it so she wouldn't have to bear the weight of having taken a life, even though their job as sorcerers entailed a lot of death.

"You guys are too nice for sorcerers."

She thought of her comrade's considerate words immediately after a fight.

Kugisaki understood how extraordinarily kind Inumaki's words were, because she had previously experienced such kindness.

◻

Kugisaki and Inumaki didn't get a much-needed rest until the next day. First, they had to transfer Tsurube and Koizumi to Jujutsu High and report on the incident.

"You two sure had a disastrous day off," Panda said.

"Salmon, salmon," Inumaki said.

"That's for sure," Kugisaki agreed, her tired shoulders slumping. "*Hmph!* I didn't get a new bag and my boot heel came off!"

They were in the break area at Jujutsu High, surrounded by second-years. Kugisaki was drinking tea. Panda and Maki had caught her between them when they came to say hi to Inumaki after he finished his report. Kugisaki thought this group seemed tighter compared to the first-years.

"Come to think of it, it's been a while since we spent time together, probably because of my schedule," Maki said. Her chin was resting on her hands, and she was staring at Kugisaki.

Kugisaki nodded back. "Yeah. It's been about a week or two?"

"Yes, something like that," Maki replied. Looking at Kugisaki's face, she realized something. As did Panda. And Inumaki, of course. There could be no doubt about it.

Kugisaki blinked at their staring faces and said, "Is there something in my teeth?"

"You look better since we last met," Maki said.

"Oh, you can tell? I bought a good foundation," Kugisaki responded.

"What I meant is you look more like a sorcerer," Maki explained. "If we were to spar now, the results might be different than last time."

Before summer, everyone had thought of Kugisaki as a mere sprout, but a series of challenges—sudden realizations, some under duress, and relationships with others—can cause a flower to bloom. Kugisaki might've still been green, but she was rapidly maturing. Even now, the flower that was Nobara Kugisaki was continuing to bloom. The second-years could clearly sense the change because they had trained with her.

Kugisaki looked uncomfortable with the compliment. She glanced at Inumaki, who was beside Panda, and dropped her eyes. "No, you shouldn't compliment me."

"Why not? You're not usually so humble," Maki said.

Kugisaki looked at Inumaki and said, "That whole incident was—"

"Fish flakes," Inumaki said, cutting her off. He had witnessed her growth with his own eyes. More than anyone here, he wanted her to be proud of herself.

"Inumaki Senpai," Kugisaki said.

"Kelp," he said.

"Okay... I won't be so humble."

"Salted fish roe," he replied.

"Yeah, it's creepy to me too," Kugisaki retorted, "But do you have to harp on it?"

"Spicy cod roe."

"Hey, you don't have to go *that* far!" Kugisaki snapped. Inumaki's high spirits were causing him to get a bit carried away, and the break area resounded with their chatter.

"Nobara, maybe you understand Toge a little *too* well now?" Panda asked, tilting his head. He supposed that was another sign of growth.

The older students looked warmly on their charming but sharp-tongued young apprentice.

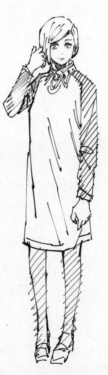

Nobara
Kugisaki

2014.12.08

CHAPTER 2 Even if I'm Not Here

CHAPTER 2 Even if I'm Not Here

When people are born, the name they receive is a kind of wish. It was unclear what kind of wish had been imbued in the name Kokichi, but Kokichi Muta knew that wish was fragile.

Heaven doesn't bestow only blessings. It had given him cursed energy but not freedom. It would have been great if his immense strength brought happiness, but it didn't, so he had no choice but to consider it a curse instead of a blessing.

Heavenly Restriction meant Kokichi Muta had to sacrifice a healthy and sound body in exchange for his power. Even moonlight burned his sensitive skin. He was missing part of his right arm and his legs, and he was connected to a life-support system, which meant he couldn't even leave his dim room.

In return, he had a massive amount of cursed energy and a cursed technique with a wide range. This exchange, to which he had never agreed, had been set since his birth. In this dark room that allowed no freedom, Kokichi Muta sought release in the fantasies of television. Otherwise, he might have gone insane.

One robot anime had made a particular impression on him. It was made for children, but the machinery and dim light of the robots' cockpit had reminded him of his own environment. Imagining himself as the mechanized hero portrayed in a work of fiction was his only consolation.

The anime told an epic story about a steel-clad hero who could never break. Missiles shot through the air burning hotter than hellfire, and the robotic punches were faster than wind. In their confrontations, the robots' bodies creaked and shed sparks.

One robot would yield to neither sword nor bullets. No matter the damages he suffered nor the burdensome fate he bore, he would not bend. He fought like a storm, got back up over and over again, and always returned to his comrades.

That robot was called...

"Mechamaru, you've got a glow! Have you changed your foundation?" Mai asked.

"Of course not. Panda demolished me, so now I'm brand new," Mechamaru replied.

"You make it sound almost heartwarming," said Miwa.

They were in the second-year classroom at Kyoto Jujutsu High School. Mechamaru was checking the condition of the joints in his right hand.

"That panda just isn't cute," said Mai. "He acts like an old dude."

"Well, Panda was a gorilla, not a panda," Mechamaru explained.

"As if that makes any sense," replied Miwa.

"Did you attend a Goodwill Event at Ueno Zoo or something?" Mai asked.

"All right, quiet down now," Assistant Manager Tanabe said, ending their conversation with a clap of his hands.

Tanabe turned off the lights and used a projector to show images of traffic accidents on the white wall. They were a sharp contrast to the Japanese-style architecture defining the room's interior. Judging from Tanabe's puffed-up demeanor, Mai and Mechamaru guessed that he chose this room because of the importance of the meeting, so they were attentive.

"It has become clear that the outbreak of traffic accidents around Kyoto is the work of a curse user," Tanabe said.

"A curse user? Not a cursed spirit?" Miwa asked.

"Well, witnesses have spotted a cursed spirit with an unnatural appearance at some of the crash sites," Tanabe explained. "It was a shikigami, which led to suspicion that the curse user was purposely disturbing drivers of motor vehicles. I investigated, and..." Tanabe switched images. Now they were looking at an overhead view of Kyoto. Indicators marked the locations of a few accidents. "Judging from the accident sites and residuals, there is a high possibility that the curse user's hideout is *here*."

"Mount Hiei?" Mai asked, frowning as she recognized the location.

It wasn't unthinkable. Well-known historical locations were prime sites for negative emotions. The burnt remains of Enryaku Temple on Mount Hiei are well-known. It's said that Oda Nobunaga's slaughter of the Buddhist priests there spared neither young nor old, man nor woman, not even children. The severity of that incident led to it becoming a famous paranormal site.

Mai tilted her head. "Seriously? A little obvious, no?"

"Yes, it's suspicious. I agree." Tanabe nodded. "Ordinarily, a curse user would be unable to hide on Mount Hiei, an area that sorcerers treat with extra caution because it's a good spot for cursed spirits to gather. Jujutsu High personnel frequently visit Enryaku Temple, and they wouldn't fail to notice any suspicious individuals or evidence."

"But they did."

"And there's a reason for that," Tanabe said.

"Is this connected to that news story a couple months ago?" Mechamaru asked.

"You are correct, Mr. Ultimate."

"Ultimate isn't my last name."

Mechamaru heard a tittering of voices. With a scraping of metal on metal, he turned to face them. Miwa was still laughing, but Mai got the conversation back on course to avoid any further disagreement on the matter.

"Surely it's not the place with the toxic gas eruption."

"Yes, that's the place," Tanabe answered. "An automotive dealer from Shiga Prefecture had a maintenance facility there, where they stored damaged cars. It filled up with toxic exhaust fumes, then someone put a curtain there."

"So now sorcerers can't go in to fight because of the gas, and humans can't go in to resolve the gas issue because of the curtain," Mechamaru reasoned.

"I doubt the gas issue would resolve on its own—the curtain is probably keeping it in. But it is possible to go in and investigate, right?"

"Yeah, you could use gas masks or a reconnaissance shikigami."

"But since human beings couldn't go in without special equipment, no one suspected a curse user was hiding there. I guess that's why the higher-ups didn't do anything sooner. Thus, the gas stayed there, and when you went to investigate, there was a curtain."

"That's right," Tanabe said. Seeing Miwa and Mai work it out for themselves left him feeling less important.

"Do we have any info on the curse user? Like their power level or cursed technique?"

"The cursed technique is probably simple manipulation of objects using shikigami as a medium. If we restrict the target for manipulation to the functioning of automobiles, we may be able to estimate the cursed technique's range and force. Having said that, we can speculate from the broad range of the cursed technique that the curse user is semi-grade 1 or higher."

"That doesn't tell us much."

"Well, we have to guess based on the evidence from the accidents around the city. Furthermore, the gas is covering a large area and there's only so much we can do with shikigami. A thorough investigation would take time we don't have because then the curse user might get away. We have to go straight in, prepared to eliminate or capture the offender."

"But the poisonous gas is an obvious obstacle, and without knowing the curse user's rank, what can we do? Besides, isn't assigning this to Jujutsu High School students a bit..." Miwa broke off and looked at Mechamaru.

"As you seem to have guessed," Tanabe said, "Kyoto Jujutsu High has a sorcerer who is able to use a cursed technique to cover a broad area remotely. It makes him suitable for the mission."

"So it's Mechamaru's mission and his alone?"

"Basically, yes. I did think, however, that I would ask you two to help me keep an eye on the city."

"Grunt work," Mai grumbled, still looking at Mechamaru.

Mechamaru's expression hadn't changed, because he didn't have a function for facial expressions. By contrast, Mai looked displeased and Miwa's face revealed the opposite of easy acceptance. No one needed to ask how the others were feeling.

"No problem. I'm the one best suited to the job," Mechamaru said indifferently.

It was still early for bright autumn foliage, but the edges of the leaves in the school courtyard were beginning to turn. Kokichi liked seeing the Kyoto school through the human-sized Mechamaru as opposed to the smaller puppet he used for side jobs. Unfortunately, seeing the world from inside a puppet created a sense of separation, like looking through glass. However, he had no choice at the moment, so he had given up on anything better, for the time being, at least.

"My objective is to seize control of the curse user's base of operations," Mechamaru said.

Even if I'm Not Here

The sorcerers could probably have easily suppressed the base with superior numbers, inundating it with a fighting force of as many puppets as they could muster, including Mechamaru. However, the spares registered at Jujutsu High were active as informers, so they needed to remain secret. Besides, it was preferable to keep the puppets, including the heavy hitters, on standby, so that they could collectively intercept attacks by special grade cursed spirits.

Kokichi knew that secrets could come back to bite you, but he wouldn't truly realize the impact of that truth until later.

"Mechamaru," a voice called out to him.

Mechamaru had been so focused on the scenery that he hadn't noticed someone approaching.

"Oh...Kamo?" he said.

"You don't appear to have any lasting effects from the Goodwill Event," Kamo said.

"I wasn't the one who got injured."

"You have a point there."

Kamo's attitude wasn't particularly apologetic. What caught Mechamaru's attention was that the boy hadn't removed the bandage from his head.

"Are you okay?" he asked.

"No worries," Kamo replied. "It's not so bad I can't walk around."

Mechamaru was unable to brush off Kamo's reply with small talk. There had been a deal that was supposed to ensure the Kyoto students were protected from harm, but then special grade cursed spirits attacked. There was no way it could have been predicted, but Kokichi himself had undoubtedly been a contributing factor. Kamo's injury was just one result of Kokichi's actions.

Mechamaru was unable to show emotion, which helped Kokichi hide how he felt. He couldn't hide silence, however, which Kamo interpreted as concern.

"Don't be so dramatic," he said. "I can even play baseball. There's really no need to worry."

"That's right," Mechamaru replied. "The second day of the

Goodwill Event was a baseball competition."

"I thought it was a bad joke."

"Satoru Gojo always keeps things lively."

"You can say that again."

Kamo's expression betrayed little, but to Mechamaru's eyes, he seemed more amused than usual, as if something good had happened.

That reminded Mechamaru of something he wanted to ask about. "I heard they used a pitching machine instead of me."

Mechamaru had seen it in action through the eyes of a small surveillance puppet. He'd raised the topic because he felt sad at having been unable to participate openly. He had wanted to feel as if at least a shadow of himself was present at the boisterous social event, but Kamo was silent and looked uncomfortable.

"Um, I wasn't being critical," Mechamaru added.

"Iori Sensei said that if we were going to do it, we should use our best lineup and aim for victory," Kamo replied.

"He gets a little strange when it comes to sports and Satoru Gojo."

"Yes, he's like that."

Kamo stood beside Mechamaru and gazed at the same trees. The breeze brushed at their cheeks. After a silence, Kamo said, "I heard you're going to investigate Mount Hiei."

"That didn't take long," Mechamaru replied.

"Unless it's top secret, word travels fast around this small school."

"It isn't a major mission. A curse user is hiding in some poisonous gas. Toxins can't affect me, so the fastest way to resolve it is for me to go."

"Acting on that assumption could put you in danger."

"Even if the unexpected happens and I take damage—"

"Mechamaru," Kamo interrupted, "this involves the transportation grid, which is part of the city's infrastructure, like water and electricity. Many curse users who attack such targets also make a living by taking on assassination jobs. If we take too long to investigate, there could be considerable losses. You should be proud that they chose you for the mission."

"Why are you so full of praise all of a sudden?"

"I suspect you view Mechamaru as expendable equipment."

"Well, it's a fact."

"Yes. The destruction of that body wouldn't threaten your own life, so you can charge into situations with the intention of boldly seizing victory. You're particularly suited to missions like this one. However, if you get too accustomed to fighting with no risk of death, you might let down your guard and eventually do something careless that would cause you to lose everything."

Kokichi knew that Kamo's criticism was often spot-on. It was especially applicable now after his fight against Panda at the Goodwill Event. After using Ultimate Cannon, Mechamaru had been so certain of victory that he'd allowed Panda to come too close.

"And then there's Mai," Kamo went on.

"What about Mai?"

"Miwa was pretty upset when she saw you get destroyed."

"Well, she wasn't born into a sorcerer family. She'll never be able to handle this job if she gets upset over the destruction of a mere physical form."

"But Mai and Miwa spend their days with that physical form."

"What's your point?"

"I'm asking you to be careful. It wouldn't take much for that body to be destroyed," Kamo said. He turned and began heading back the way he had come. "Even that body isn't alone in the world."

Kokichi couldn't see Kamo's face as he walked away. He felt like calling out to Kamo, but he couldn't find the right words to express the feelings arising within him. They got all tangled up and then they disappeared.

No longer in the mood to gaze at scenery, Mechamaru walked down the hall toward the dorm. Sometimes, this action struck Kokichi as unusual. When he had first begun using the robot Mechamaru as a body, it had been a thrill—it was like in an anime—but living this way was unnatural. Mechamaru was a body that moved around Jujutsu High, but it wasn't interchangeable with the sorcerer controlling it. Kokichi hadn't set one foot outside the room that held his life-support system.

Mechamaru had been assigned a dorm room simply because it was an efficient space for storing a human-sized object. Even though Kokichi understood that intellectually, the act of returning Mechamaru to his dorm room felt more like parking a remote-control car in a garage than a real human action.

Nonetheless, he had paid attention to the interior decoration, so he had a pleasant space where he could enjoy private time and watch television. He supposed it was similar to how a normal human might chill with a screen playing video games. It felt relaxing, so he returned to his room whenever he had free time, much like any other student.

On this day he did not reach his room without incident.

Aoi Todo, a man who seemed peculiar even to Mechamaru, was staring out the hallway window. His large build seemed even larger when he was indoors, and for a moment Mechamaru thought he was encountering a bear.

Todo had his own way of impressing himself on others, and he could be quite intimidating. He would be a fierce and troublesome opponent, and he was a reassuring and troublesome ally. When a pitch struck him during the baseball game at the Goodwill Event, members of both teams had praised the pitcher.

There was a part of Kokichi that recoiled from Todo's forceful physical presence. The large boy had handled himself well during the recent intrusion by special grade cursed spirits, but Kokichi still felt pity for him—as if Mechamaru was in any position to take pity on others.

Todo's foul temper today did not seem to stem from baseball.

"What's wrong? Why do you look so glum?" Mechamaru asked.

"I messed up the recording," Todo answered.

"What recording?"

"Takada was going to appear on a travel show on the day of the Goodwill Event."

"Oh, right. You mentioned that."

Todo had refused Principal Gakuganji's words and stormed off. It wasn't particularly unusual, but Kokichi had thought at the time that it was irresponsible.

"Maybe the Blu-Ray recorder at the Tokyo school was a piece of junk or the invasion by the cursed spirits messed it up, but I set the recorder and it didn't work!"

"Didn't you record it at the dorm?"

"Do you think I'd mess up recording in my own home? That one turned out all right, of course!"

A vein was already bulging on Todo's forehead, so Kokichi chose his next words carefully. "Then what's the problem?"

"You shoot beams from your hands, right? So you must know about the Taka-Tan Beam."

"I've never heard of it."

"How is that possible? Don't you take beams seriously?"

If Mechamaru had possessed moveable features, he might have scowled in offense at Todo's anger. Sometimes he was grateful for his unresponsive face. "I'll look it up."

"The Taka-Tan Beam is Takada's trademark pose. Make sure you do look it up, because she'll probably display it on the quiz show she's appearing on the day after tomorrow."

"Okay. So what does this have to do with anything?"

"At the precise moment that she did the Taka-Tan Beam on a TV show, a message showed up onscreen about a terrorist attack in

Kyoto traffic. Considering the timing, it may have been that mysterious curse user..."

Kokichi couldn't tell if Todo was being facetious or if he was seriously concerned. However, the vein throbbing on his forehead wasn't normal. He was so angry that to describe his state as agitated would be an understatement.

"The curse user you're gonna go take out," Todo clarified.

"It would seem my mission has become common knowledge," Mechamaru said.

"You gotta waste that curse user's ass! Their antics are causing damage all over the city, *and* they ruined Takada's big moment!"

Kokichi realized that Todo was being serious, but he wasn't particularly relieved about it. Perhaps that discomfort showed in his posture, because Todo raised his eyebrows.

"Aren't you serious about this mission?" Todo asked.

"Yes, I'm serious," Mechamaru answered.

"Then answer me this. What type of girl do you like?"

"What does that have to do with anything?!"

Todo heaved a sigh. "Well, you carry an awfully heavy burden this time..."

Kokichi knew Todo had skills. Compared to Kamo, however, who was a better sorcerer in both skill and demeanor, Todo's behavior was strange and incomprehensible. Kokichi sometimes said things that irritated him, and it was frustrating to disappoint him without knowing why.

"What do you mean?" Mechamaru asked.

"A person's sexuality explains everything about them. But you haven't answered my question. You have an inclination, but you're hiding it! If you can't just come out and say it, you're not a sorcerer!"

"How does that make any sense?!"

"It does! A man who can't stand proud will never reign triumphant!" With no further explanation, Todo stomped off down the hallway.

Well, if I had a flesh-and-blood body, maybe I wouldn't be so hesitant, Kokichi thought.

He considered the matter. Even if he had been fully flesh and blood, there was no reason he should have to tell Todo his preferences when it came to women. Todo could be persuasive with his rhetoric, but Kokichi didn't think his reasoning actually made any sense in this case. Still, Kokichi couldn't help but feel a little guilty. Todo had touched on something sensitive, and Kokichi suspected that if he had answered, they might have had a meaningful conversation about it.

The day came for Mechamaru's investigatory mission to Mount Hiei. The skies were gray and drizzling. While he couldn't sense the atmospheric temperature dropping with the rain, he could feel his metal fingers stiffening. It was inconvenient, but at least it was a new experience.

The mission was set to begin in the afternoon. Mechamaru waited near the vending machines at Jujutsu High for the car that would take him to the mountain. This body couldn't drink soda or coffee, but he enjoyed seeing students using their break time to have a beverage. He wanted to be like them.

"Oh! Here you are, Mechamaru!" a voice called out.

"Miwa? What do you need?"

Mechamaru lifted his head and saw Mai and Nishimiya as well. They were a tight-knit trio at the Kyoto campus, and he often saw them together, even though they weren't all in the same grade. But why were they approaching him now?

He recalled how once, Mai and Nishimiya had gotten carried away and convinced Miwa to give him a double A battery for Valentine's Day. They had told her that he had a taste for EVOLTA brand batteries. This had bothered him, and he had wondered if they had eaten something that made them act that way.

Even aside from such hijinks, these three were like the incarnation of mischief. People from other prefectures said Kyoto women were frightening, and even though Kokichi didn't know much about the world, he could understand what they meant.

"Mechamaru, hold out your hand," Nishimiya said.

She was a senior student, so it was difficult to refuse. Mechamaru wasn't certain which hand to offer, but eventually he held out his right hand. Miwa pulled something from her pocket, thrust it toward his wrist joint where it wouldn't interfere with his armament, and affixed it there.

"What is this?"

Mechamaru's face couldn't change expressions, but in his room, Kokichi's eyes widened.

It was a cheap scrunchie. That in itself wasn't surprising, but there was a keychain swinging from it—was it the style of character design called "SD" for "super deformed"? The keychain was a capsule toy of a small character, the type whose head and body are the same size. The soft plastic had been painted to look like metal armor. It looked like a robot.

Mai snickered at the sight of a robot decorating a robot. "The three of us went shopping yesterday," she said. "We went to the sixth floor of Avanti, where we don't get to go very often."

"Avanti? Where is that?" Mechamaru asked, cocking his head. Since he rarely went out, he didn't know of it.

Nishimiya answered, "It's on Hachi-jo Street near Kyoto Station. Mai said she wanted to play the pistol-shooting game at an arcade there."

"I never said that!" Mai insisted.

"It was surprisingly fun. I've never seen a place outside of Akihabara with so many capsule toys!" Miwa said.

"But they're more expensive than you think," Nishimiya said. "You can't get too into them. I got obsessed with these ugly-but-cute cat keychains and ended up blowing a bunch of money."

"I realized Momo is the type who should never play pachinko," Mai said.

"Don't make me sound so seedy, Mai!" Nishimiya chided with a pout.

Mai stifled a laugh.

Kokichi thought about how nice it was to have peers.

"Anyway, we stumbled across these capsule toys. We were surprised to see they had Mechamaru ones!" Nishimiya said.

"Yes, I'm surprised too," Mechamaru replied.

Of course, the keychain didn't look like Ultimate Mechamaru. It portrayed a more heroic robot from a well-known anime. In fact, it was the iconic robot in the anime that Kokichi, who operated Mechamaru, had once admired and been so crazy about. It was the source of his highest aspirations.

"Mai said we definitely had to use it to decorate you," Miwa said, at which Mai covered her mouth and laughed.

"It's all right, isn't it?" Mai asked. In English, she said, *"Mechamaru on Mechamaru. It suits you! Bwa ha ha!"*

"It's not that funny, Mai," Miwa said. "Besides, is 'on' even the right English preposition there?"

Mechamaru raised his right arm and looked at the robot character dangling on its chain. At that moment, the wind changed and the clouds parted. The sudden brightening of the sun made Kokichi squint.

"It's time, Mechamaru," Assistant Manager Tanabe called from the other side of the hall.

Caressing his right arm as if it were precious, Mechamaru lowered his sleeve, covering his new ornament.

"See you later!"

Mechamaru had already turned his back, so he couldn't see the speaker's expression. However, the tone of voice and the emotion it carried resounded through him.

"Thank you. I'll be back," Kokichi said. As he spoke, he realized his words sounded like a promise to return to his schoolmates.

The trees passing by the car window resembled a person racing through life. Tanabe and Kokichi's destination had once been a public facility, so it could be reached by car; however, given that the curse user's cursed technique involved controlling automobiles, it might not be wise to drive too close. For that reason, Mechamaru decided he would disembark partway there and walk the rest of the not-inconsiderable distance to the site. Tanabe looked apologetic and had trouble accepting this decision, but Mechamaru told him not to worry about it.

This was no time for enjoying the scenery, but the colorful mountains caught Kokichi's attention. Under the trees, whose leaves blocked the rain, a bird that looked like it was wearing a little necktie hopped over a carpet of fallen leaves. That was a Japanese tit, Tanabe had said as they passed, and Kokichi had turned over the name in his head.

Now Mechamaru walked along a route he had studied beforehand. A faint wind was blowing, and it was raining. Birds took shelter in the trees and insects crawled under fallen leaves.

Kokichi hadn't set a foot outside his room, so all he could do was gaze out through Mechamaru's eyes, but that was how he interacted with the world. If his body healed, would he be able to experience nature and its countless life-forms with his own senses?

Come to think of it, that gorilla-like panda had said he would come to visit Kokichi. Panda himself didn't have the kind of physical form that could just go gallivanting around in the open, so Kokichi wondered how he intended to visit. Panda looked so much like a panda that he didn't even wear clothes the way Mechamaru did. Kokichi tried to picture Panda wearing a hoodie, jeans, and a hat to board the bullet train. If he did it boldly, he just might get away with it. Kokichi surprised himself by smiling, but he knew this daydream would never come to pass. He didn't know what to call the feeling arising within him, so he pondered it for a moment.

That was careless.

As he reached a crossroads, he suddenly heard an engine. A red sedan with a bent license plate was glaring at him. It took off toward him, racing down the slope of the road, a metal box accelerating under the force of gravity. Its trajectory was simple, but its area and mass made it a threat.

Mechamaru had no choice but to take drastic evasive action. He was in the mountains, so he could dive into the trees to avoid a collision. Still on a course for Mechamaru, the sedan slammed into a tree and stopped. Mechamaru watched as the crash caused birds to burst from branches.

"What a welcome," Mechamaru said.

He stayed off the road as he continued through the trees toward his destination. Since the enemy was deploying a considerable attack, he would be safer with obstacles around. However, the closer he drew to the curse user's base, the fewer obstacles there would be.

As he walked, a change came over the branches of the trees around him. The leaves were dead and black instead of green tinged with red. Previously, everything had taken on a white cast in the drizzle, but now it seemed murky because of the gas. Eventually the trees thinned out, the view opened up, and he entered an open area.

The scene before him looked like an automobile graveyard. Some vehicles retained their original form, while others were nothing but piles of junk. Deep in his gas-obscured field of vision, beyond a mound of scrap metal, Mechamaru saw a building that looked like a factory.

"Would a curse user hide in a factory?" he wondered.

Abandoned cars surrounded the area, which, given the curse user's technique, put Mechamaru at a disadvantage. The curse user was likely to notice any intruder who stood there gawking, and

Mechamaru wouldn't be surprised if the enemy used that moment to escape.

But to catch a lion cub, you had to enter the lion's den, so Mechamaru remained on high alert and advanced into the junkyard. His metal humanoid form traversed this labyrinth of abandoned cars, a forest of rusted, decrepit steel. It was like a graveyard full of black gas, showing no signs of life. Aside from his own heavy footfalls, it was eerily silent.

Kokichi was considering the significance of the quiet when a small form darted in between abandoned cars. It was a remote control car, he realized. It was making a faint noise as it raced along. A shikigami was riding in it, sitting next to a box-shaped device that the curse user had apparently strapped into where the seats were.

Kokichi had known that the enemy's cursed technique involved manipulating automobiles, so he had expected that the curse user would use the mass of full-sized cars to crush him to death. This curse user, however, appeared to be able to employ a variety of modern technologies.

Mechamaru pointed his arm toward the remote control car. "What a small target!" he exclaimed.

His left palm opened, revealing the device that fired the Ultra Cannon. Suppressing the output, Mechamaru immediately found his aim and fired. The blast struck, and the remote control car went up in flames. The next moment, there was a bright flash and an explosion much larger than what could have been generated by a mere battery-powered toy.

"I suspected as much. Explosives!" Mechamaru remarked.

Mechamaru planted both feet on the ground to withstand the blast. Just then, he spotted two—no, *three* remote control cars racing toward him, using the roofs of the abandoned cars as ramps to launch themselves across the junkyard. Mechamaru had been careful to restrict the Ultra Cannon's output, but he still barely had time to reload. In the nick of time, he brought up his hand and fired again.

Even at reduced output, Ultra Cannon wasn't supposed to fire consecutive shots, but Mechamaru mowed down the remote control cars anyway, swinging his arm without bothering to brace against the recoil.

"It seems the curse user has prepared considerable defenses," he commented.

Kokichi was beginning to sense the gravity of the situation. He couldn't possibly defend against exploding remote control cars with close-range armaments like Sword Option and Ultra Shield. Thus, he had no choice but to shoot. As he rapidly alternated between cooling and firing, though, the burden on his arm was mounting. Furthermore, a remote control car exploded near him, and the blast limited the space in which he could maneuver. Mechamaru had saved armament for use later, but that put him at a disadvantage against an enemy this relentless with their attacks.

Mechamaru exercised direct control over puppets. In the case of a cursed technique that used shikigami as the substrate for controlling machines, however, the number of shikigami was limited to the number of cars the curse user could control at any particular moment. That meant there had to be a break in the attacks. When that break came, Mechamaru could follow the route by which the shikigami returned to the curse user and pinpoint their master's location. However, Kokichi decided that focusing on withstanding the enemy's attacks was wisest for the time being.

Just then, from beyond the flames of the explosions from the remote control cars, a giant shadow fell across the mountain of abandoned cars. A tanker truck was hurtling toward Mechamaru.

"So that's how it is, huh?!" he exclaimed.

The essence of the enemy's cursed technique was that the curse user could manipulate any kind of automobile, and that leeway allowed for a broad range of attacks. The explosions had maneuvered Mechamaru into a position where he would have little room to evade the falling tanker. Even if he did so, he might lose an arm or a leg.

Mechamaru needed to take out the curse user who was deploying the shikigami. He was almost overheating, but since he didn't have many long-range attacks, he couldn't afford to lose Ultra Cannon. Preserving his left arm was necessary for victory.

Having made his decision, Mechamaru evaded in a way that could result in losing his right arm instead. However, he hesitated.

In the next instant, there was an explosion several times more powerful than the explosions from the remote control cars. The blast burned Mechamaru's uniform and sent him flying. He ended up rolling on the ground.

He had used his all-important left arm to shield himself from the powerful blast and ended up sacrificing it in the process. Without even realizing it, he had protected his right arm.

"Aw..." he muttered.

The burnt sleeve now exposed Mechamaru's right wrist, causing him to realize why he had moved in such an irrational way. The keychain on the scrunchie attached to his right arm rattled as it dangled there.

"It appears you have realized your mistake," a voice said.

"Must be the curse user..." Mechamaru speculated.

The voice was coming from the stereo of a nearby abandoned car. Though indistinct, it suggested someone younger than Mechamaru had imagined. The curse user didn't sound worried. They knew that Mechamaru had messed up.

Kokichi bit his scabbed lips—he really had messed up. He had succumbed to an emotional attachment that had no place in battle, and that was careless. The common affairs of everyday life were like a curse that had limited his power. Nonetheless, the curse user pointing out his error caused him to seethe with anger.

"I'm surprised they sent a cursed corpse, but I guess it makes sense," the curse user said. "You're remote control, like my cursed technique. You misunderstood my cursed technique, though. The only thing I can use are small insect-like shikigami. Within my field of vision, if I have the shikigami possess an object like a car, I can control almost all of that car's functions and do whatever I want with its mounted cameras and navigation systems."

"You planned on divulging your cursed technique. That's why you left the car navigation systems operational," Mechamaru guessed.

"Impressive," the curse user replied. "It's gratifying to have someone with a bit of theory to appreciate my methods."

Kokichi ground his teeth. The curse user had gotten the better of him; it was only natural that he would boast about it.

The problem was that the curse user had chosen this particular moment to reveal his cursed technique. He had even provided a clue to his location with the words "within my field of vision." That suggested the curse user meant to finish off Mechamaru right here and now instead of running away—although Kokichi supposed he might also render Mechamaru immobile and then flee at his leisure. At any rate, he was certain that Mechamaru was his only opponent.

Kokichi thought it through. The curse user was probably located somewhere that afforded an overhead view of the entire junkyard. Kokichi should be able to determine where that was.

Mechamaru raised his gaze past the top floor of the abandoned factory to the roof. He spotted a figure wearing a gas mask and an air tank. The man, who looked more like a mad scientist than a curse user, was looking down at him.

"Ah, our eyes meet," the man said. "You've got me in your sights."

"Yet you don't sound worried," Mechamaru replied.

"Because I'm not. You've located me, but you don't show any intention of attacking. No more long-distance moves, perhaps?"

"Aren't you perceptive?"

"Yes...perception is what drivers need most. Look right, look left, look right again. And be sure to look over your shoulder. One must obey the rules of the road, sorcerer."

"Well, my real body is immobile. I can only use remote-control bodies, so I don't get out much."

Mechamaru had no way of attacking during this conversation. He had lost Ultra Cannon when he lost his left arm, and without it, even with a visual lock on the enemy, he couldn't execute a long-range attack. As the enemy prepared for the crushing blow, Mechamaru felt helpless.

No, I can do something, he thought.

He could go all-or-nothing with Mode: Albatross. That was the artillery in his mouth for Ultimate Cannon. However, Ultimate Cannon ordinarily required the support of both arms, and his body was damaged. The most he would be able to manage before overheating was one shot.

Nonetheless, his chances of taking out the curse user weren't low. Judging by the air tank the curse user wore, he was a shiki-gami user and typical of the type—meaning he himself wasn't much good in a fight.

Thus, the chances of Mechamaru striking his target were high. If he could manage a long-range attack, he could probably finish the fight, but it would result in this body's destruction. But there was no reason to hold back when using disposable equipment.

Kokichi knew that was his smartest option. Despite that, however, Mechamaru swung his right arm and extended the blade called Sword Option. Deploying a close-range weapon in this situation was like an admission of the futility of his situation.

"What can you do with a blade from over there?" the curse user asked.

"I can strike you down," Mechamaru replied.

"Impossible. Are you so foolish that you don't know why I've pushed you to exactly that spot?"

"No, I do know. But I want to make this hard for you."

Mechamaru glanced around the area. The small shikigami, which looked like mosquitoes, disappeared into the mountain of scrap cars.

"Once I've killed you, you'll be just another piece of scrap," the curse user declared.

Mechamaru lunged with Sword Option. At the same moment, flames erupted throughout the mountain of automobiles. The curse user must have used shikigami to blow up a large amount of explosive material somewhere inside it. Scrap rained down, blocking escape in any lateral direction, but that didn't prevent movement in every direction, for Mechamaru's blade was homing in on a specific object.

The curse user shouted when he realized Mechamaru's target.

When the tanker had fallen, one of its enormous tires had come off. The blast from such a large tire when it ruptures can be greater than that of a grenade. Kokichi Muta himself was missing part of his right arm and both his legs. That he had tried to protect Mechamaru's right arm, which wasn't really his, had been foolish, but there was something he could do with that arm now, precisely because it was mechanical—and equipped with a blade.

Mechamaru swung at the tire. The force of it bursting, aided by the blasts from other explosions, carried Mechamaru high into the air.

"Boost on! Maximum output!" he shouted.

The booster from his right elbow activated, giving him even more altitude. His right arm, however, began to fail due to damage from the tire exploding and stress on the boosters that had been propelling him.

"Come on, come on..." Mechamaru muttered.

When he reached a point higher than the factory, he used his mouth to rip the keychain from his right arm. Even that action further eroded his arm. At the zenith of his arc, he experienced a moment of weightlessness, then twisted his body and swung his near-demolished arm downward.

"*Tch!*" The curse user realized what Mechamaru was aiming for and began to flee, but it was too late.

At the Goodwill Event, Mechamaru had carelessly turned his back on Panda, and this scene now played in Kokichi's head. His certainty in finishing the fight with a big move had caused him to permit an opening.

Choosing this particular tactic might have been irrational. Perhaps it was too sentimental for someone who had joined hands with cursed spirits to want to bring this body home from a fight. He wanted that more than ever, however, when he looked at the cheap keychain. These irrational feelings fueled Kokichi's cursed energy.

"You should have kept your shikigami nearby for defense," Mechamaru said.

If obsession gave rise to curses, then sorcerers could change curses into strength. Mechamaru fired his boosters at the same time he swung, packing his right arm with maximum force.

A scene from the anime Kokichi used to watch flashed in the back of his mind. It was a powerful signature move, and everyone who admired robots knew about it. A steel fist launching and flying through the air...

"*Rocket Punch!*"

Like a dark gray shooting star, it parted the cloud of gas. Launched at high speed, his fist assumed the momentum of a cannon ball. Mechamaru often used firearms and projectiles, so his aim with this long-range attack was sure to be accurate.

If the curse user had been more agile, he could have dodged, but he was a shikigami user in a respirator. He made a desperate attempt to loose his shikigami, but he was too late. Mechamaru's fists were faster than wind.

"*Uaaaarrrrrgggghhhhh!*" The shikigami user's scream, muffled by the gas mask, sounded from the stereos of several abandoned cars.

When Mechamaru's fist struck, the explosion swallowed those screams. The shikigami frantically flitted around, losing control and plummeting to the ground. Kokichi, realizing the curse user had fallen unconscious, managed to land then, despite missing both arms.

"Oof..." he sighed.

Kokichi wondered why he had been so desperate to preserve an expendable body. What powered his steel puppet was his own desire to return home and see his friends again.

The curtain lifted and a drizzle washed away the cloud of gas. It was all over, and Mechamaru was still standing.

A pleasant blue sky stretched overhead. It was the morning after the mission. Mechamaru was sitting on a bench in the courtyard of Jujutsu High. He vaguely pondered what the clouds, white and drifting slowly overhead, resembled.

Light footfalls approached from the direction of the school building. He lowered his eyes and turned to see Miwa.

"Mechamaruuu!" she cried.

"Miwa?" he asked.

"Whaddaya mean, 'Miwa?' You went off on that mission and then never stopped by the classroom after. I was wondering what became of you!"

Mechamaru was quiet then.

"Why so silent?" Miwa asked.

"You were worried about me?"

She made an indignant face. "Of course I was!"

Kokichi figured that he would have been worried about his comrade if he had been in her position. The fight, however, had happened to a substitute body in a place outside the city. That she thought her concern about him was a matter of course awakened a funny feeling in him. Mechamaru paused before once again looking up at Miwa.

"Miwa," he said.

"Yes?" she replied.

"I'm back."

"Yeah, well...welcome back."

Kokichi felt like that brief exchange lasted an eternity. Satisfaction and a touch of sadness filled Kokichi's breast. Miwa couldn't look inside him to see his complicated feelings, so she just smiled.

"But you could've said it a little sooner," she said.

"Well, I felt awkward about it," he replied.

"Why?"

"Because the scrunchie got ripped off," he admitted.

"Oh." Miwa blinked her round eyes empathetically. "You worry about that kind of stuff, huh?"

"Is that surprising?" he asked.

"Well, I still don't know a lot about you," she replied.

"And you worry about that stuff too, huh?" he asked.

"Is that surprising?"

"Not at all," he replied.

Miwa laughed at how naturally their banter came, but Mechamaru didn't. He didn't have a function for laughing. Kokichi, however, glanced away from what Mechamaru was showing him and looked around in the dim light of his room, at piles of folded clothes. He had the burnt keychain inside a pocket.

If he told Miwa that he had been careful to bring back her gift, how would she react? He felt it would be a horrible waste to see that through Mechamaru's eyes and instead imagined what a sight that would be. Only then did he realize the importance of announcing one's return.

For that matter, how would it feel if he ever told her, "It's been nice to get to know you"? When she learned what he had done, what kind of face would she—would they all—make? He wouldn't mind if she seemed confused or displeased. He just wanted to see it with his own eyes.

"Miwa," he said.

"Yes, Mechamaru?"

I'll come see you soon. He couldn't bring himself to say it, so he just said, "Never mind."

Mechamaru didn't laugh. He didn't shed tears. But that was only because he didn't have a function for showing emotion. At that time, no one knew even that small fact about him.

Kasumi
Miwa

2019. 12.09

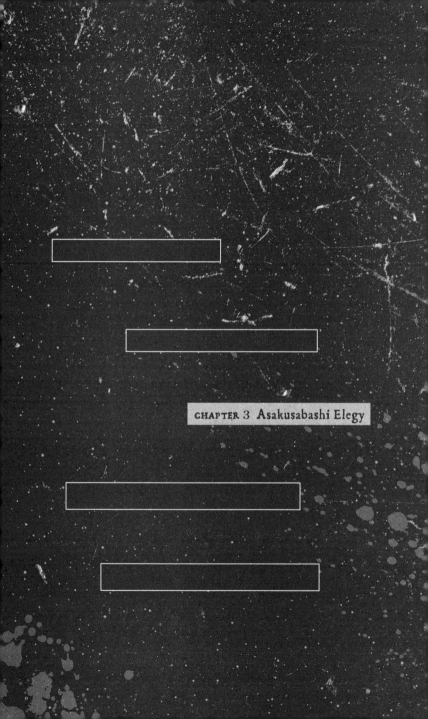

CHAPTER 3 Asakusabashi Elegy

You don't want to get older, but it happens. No one likes it, but that's reality. These days, people say you're in the prime of life in your thirties, but the reality is that once you pass twenty-five, anyone under twenty considers you old and your body begins to change.

Ill health tends to drag on. Your neck and shoulders get stiff, a kind of fever clouds your thoughts, and your bowels gurgle. Each problem on its own is no big deal, but they build up and last until the next day. And the cumulative stress hits you not when you're busy, but later, when you're trying to relax.

That's how it was for Kiyotaka Ijichi.

He sighed at this thought.

He had meetings with Kyoto Jujutsu High School to go to and paperwork related to the Kyoto Sister-School Goodwill Event to do. He had to address the matter of curse users and cursed spirits invading the school, and he had to assess the damage. He had to operate behind the scenes to replace fatalities in the ranks, and he had to tend to the families of those who hadn't survived. And he had to obtain baseball gear, which had suddenly become necessary.

Amidst all that, what was to have been his next job—a first-year mission to address damage resulting from a cursed spirit incident in

Saitama—had suddenly been assigned to a different assistant manager named Nitta. The man had even taken his investigatory data. Ever since the Goodwill Event, secrecy had shrouded the assistants' plans, so the change had come so unexpectedly that Ijichi didn't have anything prepared to replace it. His schedule hadn't been this wide open in a long time.

He let out a deflated sound when he reached his desk in the office at Jujutsu High.

Now that he thought about it, he had been working nonstop. With unexpected time on his hands, Ijichi wasn't surprised to find that his physical condition was less than desirable. He didn't do highly visible work, so he could take time off if he wanted, but it made him uncomfortable to do so except on weekends and public holidays.

Furthermore, many sorcerers were analogue-minded, while Ijichi's duties involved working on a computer and filling in online forms. Ijichi didn't like the thought of having to provide instruction over the phone if trouble requiring digital tasks arose. He knew all too well that people who were no good at computers were practically incapable of even pressing the power button.

Ijichi turned on his computer. Nothing in particular required his attention, so he checked his email and organized the icons on his desktop. Then he tweaked the forms for documents he used on a regular basis, reviewed the procedures he used for office work, and tidied up a drawer that he'd been neglecting for some time now. He had reached a stopping point and was sipping a cup of office tea when a thought came to him.

Am I just making myself more tired?

The possibility shocked him. He had thought he was working because he was busy, but now he realized that he just didn't have anything to do outside of work. It was a painful thought. He performed his duties with a sense of responsibility, but it worried him a little to imagine his life consisted of nothing more. No, it worried him a *lot*.

The sorcerers risked their lives on the front line while the most he would ever do was provide logistical support, so he didn't like to think about his own well-being. While having these thoughts, he felt a cramping sensation in his abdomen.

He sighed again.

He hadn't been overeating or drinking. He had an appetite, but for a while now he'd been feeling as though his body wasn't functioning properly. Was he tired? Yes, he was definitely tired, but he had been so absorbed in work that he hadn't noticed. He was unable to spend idle moments idly. Instead, he dragged around vague worries and found trivial tasks to fritter away the time.

This was no good. Something had to change.

"Oh, I know!"

He clapped his hands and stood up. Since his stomach hurt, he should visit the doctor! He straightened items on his desktop, locked away important documents for safekeeping, and breezily strolled to the school infirmary.

"I believe it's caused by stress. I'll prescribe a mild stomach medication."

Ijichi was at the Tokyo school's infirmary. After completing a simple examination, Shoko Ieiri offered him a bag containing powdered medication. A serious wound might have required her to perform reverse cursed technique, but that wasn't the case in this circumstance.

In an ordinary medical encounter, the doctor would perform an examination and the pharmacist would dispense medication. Ieiri, however, worked at a school infirmary. The medical facilities at Jujutsu High weren't at all like a normal school's, but it was still a school and not a hospital, so there was a limit to the kinds of procedures that could be performed there. For ailments that weren't severe, as in Ijichi's case, Ieiri had a stock of over-the-counter medications to dispense. In that way, it was no different than a common medical clinic.

"Thank you," he said. Ieiri's rudimentary physical examination had eased Ijichi's mind. "This will be an immense help."

"Your physical health seems sound," Ieiri replied, "so this is just a simple stomach remedy. It might provide you a sense of ease before social drinking. This can be found in a common drugstore. You might find some reassurance in always keeping some handy."

"Well, I thought it best to seek a professional opinion for something like this."

"A wise choice."

Ijichi sat on the stool with perfect posture and an alert expression. He was always on his best behavior. Rambunctious sorcerers were troublesome to him. Jittery sorcerers made him anxious. Sending children on missions made him feel guilty. The upper ranks gave him hell about Gojo, and of course Gojo was reckless with every breath he took. By contrast, Ieiri was a breath of fresh air. She never said anything unreasonable or expected more than he could give, and she was unaffectedly considerate.

Ijichi was used to looking at violent sorcerers and grotesque curses, so Ieiri was also a sorely needed respite for his eyes. Her complexion wasn't great, but she was without a doubt a beauty, possessed of an unusual charm. Ijichi thought her laid-back attitude made her seem mysteriously erotic.

What's more, she had been especially kind to him this time. Usually, she merely performed the necessary examination and returned to her work. On this day, however, she asked after his general health and engaged in casual chitchat.

"When I got to school and turned on my computer, the data had been reformatted," Ijichi said.

"That's too bad," Ieiri commiserated.

"It was worse than having a grade 2 cursed spirit come after me," Ijichi continued. "I realized then how important it is to keep a backup. Why worry when you can be prepared, right?"

"Like keeping a stock of blood for transfusions," Ieiri agreed.

"I suppose so, yeah."

"It's good that you've gotten over the hump now."

"I guess so," Ijichi said, but he sounded unsure. He was unusually free of obligations at the moment and was reluctantly trying to let her know that he had come to visit her in part because he didn't have anything to do. Just then, however, the fates conspired in Ijichi's favor in a way he could never have expected.

"Well," Ieiri said, "in that case, are you free tonight?"

"Huh?"

"Do you have time tonight?"

"Wha...?"

"Or would you rather I perform an otolaryngological evaluation?"

"Oh, no... I'm free, I'm free, I'm free!"

"I heard you the first time."

Ijichi's brain paused to process Ieiri's invitation. There was nothing wrong with it, but it was certainly unexpected. *Don't get any weird ideas*, he cautioned himself, but he couldn't stop from feeling rather buoyant.

Whether Ieiri had noticed his excitement was unclear. She recrossed her legs with utter composure. "Good, you're free," she said. "You should take time to go out for drinks sometimes. I thought I'd invite you."

"Um, you want to go drinking?!"

"Nothing that would upset your stomach. Although your stomach itself doesn't appear to be the problem. But a change of pace can be good for you."

"R-right. Yes, I can do that."

"Great. Let's say six o'clock in Asakusabashi. I'll tell you the name of the place later."

"Sure, got it!"

Ijichi's spine straightened even more as he answered, as if this were a job interview. Ieiri smiled faintly upon seeing his posture change. She began reorganizing medical records, a clear signal of her desire to get back to work. Ijichi didn't want to interfere, so he stood up, bowed deeply, and left.

"Well, then..." he said to himself once he had left the office.

Nothing terribly momentous had happened, but Ijichi felt a sudden rush of motivation. Now that he had plans, he couldn't work overtime. He didn't have *any* work, but just in case something came up, Ijichi raced back to his desk and began putting his affairs in order.

○

"This is the place, isn't it?"

It was 5:45. Ijichi had walked ten minutes from the Asakusabashi subway station, down a street just beginning to come alive with neon lights and salarymen coming from work, and found the designated establishment. The restaurant was called Small Bird Box, which didn't exactly inspire an appetite in someone involved with curses.

"Hmm..."

Ijichi wouldn't say the establishment he was staring at looked very appealing, either. Strung outside were red paper lanterns and a beer sign, and the entrance was a sliding door. A faint sense of excitement had been mounting in him on the journey there, but now he felt it ever so slightly receding.

"I thought we were going to have a quiet dinner alone, but..."

A faint image arose in the back of his head. Come to think of it, he had hardly ever seen Ieiri without her white coat. Ieiri was always fiddling with medication or dead bodies, and he had almost never seen her not in work mode.

As if to start his stalling engine, Ijichi took a deep breath. Then he did it again—twice, three times—replacing the air in his lungs. Having shored up his resolve, he pulled open the sliding door to the restaurant.

"Woo-hoo! You're late, Ijichi!"

Without stepping inside, Ijichi reclosed the door: *tunk!* Then he wiped his glasses with his sleeve.

Something was very wrong. Instead of Ieiri in something other than her white work coat, he had been greeted by a blond guy in sunglasses drinking melon soda from a massive mug—a guy who looked suspiciously like Gojo. Had Ijichi's eyes been cursed? Was he under attack by a brainwashing technique?

Certainly he couldn't have seen what he thought he saw.

Ieiri had invited him out. He most definitely had not come to drink with Gojo. Besides, Gojo didn't drink alcohol, so he wouldn't be in a drinking establishment like this. Perhaps exhaustion and overexcitement had caused Ijichi to hallucinate. *Yeah, that must be it.* The diligent assistant manager took another deep breath and, with great trepidation, once again opened the door.

"What gives?" the blond guy asked, looking unmistakably like Gojo.

Ijichi made a sour face as he squinted. "What are you doing, Gojo?!"

"I'm doin' nonalcoholic bondage play at a drinkin' establishment, and I ain't goin' home until I'm good and hammered!"

"Then you'll never go home."

"Well, bondage isn't any fun if you're not strapped in tight! Ijichi, are you the type who can't be satisfied until you reach high levels of kink?"

"I don't usually play those kinds of games."

"Get in here, Ijichi," a new voice said. "Gojo and I have already started."

"Oh...hi, Ieiri."

Ieiri was sitting diagonally across from Gojo at the four-person table, and she had just drained a large mug of beer.

Ijichi was beginning to comprehend the situation. Tonight's drinking session was for three. He felt something inside himself, that part of him prone to believing in dreams too good to be true, crumble with a great tumult.

This was reality. The scene before him now was much less dreamy than Ieiri inviting him, and him alone, for a drink at six o'clock. He bowed in greeting and hid his disappointment as he sat in the seat they indicated next to Gojo.

"Let's get you a first drink," Ieri said.

She summoned the server and ordered a beer for Ijichi and a highball for herself. Ijichi decided not to speculate about how many drinks she'd downed before he arrived.

The spread in front of Gojo included a melon soda, french fries, and chicken fingers, the kinds of food a small boy might order if his parents dragged him into a drinking establishment.

"All right, cheers!" Gojo said.

There was a moment of chaos as they toasted with melon soda, beer, and a highball. Then Ieiri opened a menu printed on worn Japanese paper and ordered more food. "Abalone boiled in soy sauce, chunks of raw tuna, and offal stew. Ijichi, any sides for you?"

"Um...potato salad."

"Chunky or smooth?"

"Smooth."

After swiftly completing the order, Ieiri drank from her glass with an elegant gesture. Her highball rapidly disappeared, along with the edamame and kinpira appetizers already on the table. She was guzzling her drink the way a student guzzles cold cider in the summer sun.

Her pallor was also surprising. She seemed paler than usual, so even though she had probably already finished at least one drink, she didn't look drunk or flushed. Her natural elegance combined with her capacity to drink heavily made her seem incredibly cool in Ijichi's eyes.

Meanwhile, Gojo definitely wasn't drunk, because he wasn't drinking alcohol.

"Hey, Ijichi?" Gojo said. "Did you know that Steven Spielberg was the first one to put cucumber in potato salad?"

"Oh, really? I've never heard that before."

"Yeah, cuz it isn't true," Gojo said.

"Okay..."

A conversation with a drunk would have made more sense than conversation with Gojo. That was the case whenever Gojo and Ijichi tangled, but it was even worse now. Gojo seemed to be drunk without having consumed a drop of alcohol—drunk on the atmosphere, on the convivial attitude of the crowd of daily drinkers and salarymen on their way home from work. He was acting like a bigger drinker than Ieiri.

"Ijichi," Gojo said, "since we're drinking together, let's talk about this week's issue of *Jump*!"

"I h-haven't read it."

"Seriously? There are actually people who don't read *Jump*? What did you read growing up? Or were you the intellectual who read ancient poetry in the *Kokin Wakashū*?"

"Is there an option besides *Jump* and *Kokin Wakashū*?"

"I'm appalled. Then shall we talk about baseball? Politics?"

"Huh? No, I avoid topics that provoke disagreement."

"Me? I'm a big fan of Mitsunari Ishida," Gojo said. "But I can't say he did much after Hideyoshi died."

"Politics from the Sengoku Period? That was unexpected."

"Ijichi, our precious present rests atop the deeds of our forebears."

"Yes, I know, but..."

Gojo's fine sentiment sounded as thin as a spring roll wrapper coming as it did from the very person trying to destroy the old system of the jujutsu world, but Ijichi didn't have the courage to say so.

"Y-you admire Mitsunari Ishida, do you?" Ijichi asked.

"Well, according to the stories, he always served lukewarm tea," Gojo said.

"I've never heard anyone describe a Sengoku commander like a household servant before."

"Then let's decide who would be the strongest general, regardless of the time period. I propose Satoru Gojo."

"I too think he would win."

"Yes, but Sugawara no Michizane could be a problem."

"Stop throwing around big names."

The banter was nothing new, but it was flying faster than normal. Ijichi cast a glance at Ieiri to indicate he was having trouble keeping up, but she was preoccupied.

"The tuna's here!" she said. "That means it's sake time! Waiter, what brand have you got?"

"We have Hakkaisan."

"Then that's what we'll have!"

Ieiri was ready to start knocking it back. She was the one who had chosen this restaurant, but it was still surprising to see how comfortable she was here. The way she called out to the server suggested she was a regular.

"What's wrong, Ijichi?" she said. "Have you had enough to drink?"

"Uh...yes, I have."

"Oh. Well, when the nimono gets here, don't hold back. *The chef here has serious skills!*"

"Eh? Flattery won't get you free food!" the chef called back. To the server, he said, "Prepare the usual for Shoko!"

"Comin' up, General!" the server replied.

Ijichi was taken aback when the chef called Ieiri by her first name. He wouldn't mind being able to do that himself.

"The server is new, but she's really zippy," Ieiri said. "She has four sisters-in-law, so she's holding down multiple jobs to send 'em to college. It's like something out of a manga."

"You asked her about all this?" Ijichi asked.

"Well, I've been coming here for a long time."

"Oh, I see..."

Now it made sense. Ieiri was no mere regular—she came here so often that she knew all about the servers' lives. That explained why the chef addressed her by her first name. Ijichi could accept that.

Before long, the server brought a delicious-looking shiokara, then poured sake into a glass until it overflowed into a wooden masu sake box, which in turn overflowed into a dish below it.

"That's a lot of sake!" Ijichi exclaimed.

"Usually you catch sake overflowing the glass with a masu sake box, but this restaurant pours so much it also overflows the box. It's a secret specialty called a double waterfall."

"So it's about two servings?"

"More bang for your buck, right?"

Ijichi was shocked that Ieiri could drink this much so easily, but he refrained from saying anything. "And...what's that dish that looks like shiokara?"

"Shuto," she said.

"Shuto?"

"It's shiokara made from skipjack tuna entrails. Anyway, whenever I flatter the chef, this materializes, and I've come to look forward to it. You can have some if you want."

"Oh...thank you."

"But beer isn't enough to follow it."

"Oh? Then, um..."

"A good side dish requires the right drink. Order sake and use your leftover beer as a chaser. As for me, I demand an assortment of cheese!"

"Um, all right. Sake...lukewarm."

As Ieiri was touching her lips to the rim of the glass where sake was about to overflow, Ijichi's sake arrived. Of course, none of this was going to be free. When the cheese arrived, Ieiri assembled the dishes before her with a triumphant air and explained her method.

"You put the shuto on the cheese, then follow it with sake. Try it."

Ijichi hunched, timidly following Ieiri's recommendation. "Oh, this is good. It's like drinking anchovies!"

"Told ya!" Ieiri exclaimed. "Look, Gojo! Ijichi's on my side!"

"Hunh?! I don't get all that nonsense about shiokara on cheese at all! Cheese is like a resident of the Country of Sweets that got abducted from Scone, its betrothed, and whisked away to the Country of Drunkards. Does that sound about right, Ijichi?"

"Huh? Uh...no. What?"

"Pfaw!" Ieiri scoffed. "It's your loss, teetotaler, because it totally rocks! Right, Ijichi?"

"When did Shoko get like this, Ijichi?" Gojo asked.

As Ieiri was gobbling tuna and gulping sake, Gojo was adding vanilla ice cream to his melon soda. Ijichi, caught between a woman who could drink like a fish and a child-like man with a massive sweet tooth, sipped his sake. He was afraid all this food and drink would confuse his stomach, but the sake tasted good and the food was even better, so he didn't feel that bad about it.

"The food and drink here really are good," he said.

"I always recommend this joint," Ieiri replied. "A lot of regulars bring their kids, so the restaurant also serves soft drinks and desserts. That means Gojo can come!"

"Are you treating me like a child?" Gojo asked.

"Well, you are like a big child," Ieiri replied.

As the two traded barbs, Ijichi dipped his chopsticks into the offal stew. Ieiri was right: it was delicious. The chef had cooked the meat to perfection. The pleasant miso-based seasoning had a strong taste of ginger. It was a perfect accompaniment for sake. Chopped shiso was served as an accent to the tuna, which also went excellently with sake, and the salty-sweet abalone also tempted his chopsticks. The chef's skill was undeniable.

Ijichi felt good for the first time in a long while. As time passed in a leisurely fashion, he got drunk in a leisurely fashion. The more he drank, the heavier he felt.

"Ijichi, it's been a while since you came out drinking," Ieiri said.

"Hm?" Ijichi thought back. "Now that you mention it, you're right. It has been a while. Maybe that's why the alcohol is so quick to affect me."

Gojo interrupted, slamming his mug on the table. "You're just tired!"

"But I didn't really accomplish any work worth noting today," Ijichi replied.

"Your exhaustion has been building up," Gojo insisted.

Ieiri said, "People say alcohol is the best medicine, and there's something to that! If you drink enough to feel good, you relax, and then your exhaustion hits. Ijichi, when was the last time you had any downtime?"

"Hmm..." Ijichi hadn't had any time off since the Goodwill Event. Which only made sense—it had been an unusual set of circumstances resulting in multiple deaths. He hadn't had the luxury of taking time off. He still couldn't believe he'd managed to find some free time today.

All right, then what about before the Goodwill Event?

"I told you when I examined you," Ieiri continued, "that your condition is caused by stress, but that doesn't mean it's all in your head. Stress accrues over time if you keep on working too hard and neglecting your health."

"I haven't seen you take any real time off since around July," Gojo said. "I bet you didn't take any time off at all in September."

Ijichi thought back. The sorcerer was right.

"That's true," Ijichi replied, "but we're shorthanded right now."

"Don't be stupid," Gojo said. "If you collapse because you can't recognize your limits, then we really *will* be shorthanded. Think about all the work that only you can do!"

"Huh?"

"Ijichi," Ieiri said. "It was actually Gojo who suggested taking you out tonight."

"What?!" The shock was enough to dispel Ijichi's drunkenness. He turned to gawk at Gojo.

"He wants you to realize how exhausted you are before you collapse," Ieiri said. "Are you so moved you could cry?"

"Moved? I'm astounded beyond all belief!"

Ijichi took a swig of lukewarm sake to stop himself from shaking. Then he swung his gaze from one side of the table to the other until his eyes rested on the surface of a puddle of sake that remained in his cup. He could faintly see his reflection.

"Do I really look that tired?" he asked.

"I knew it was serious when you tried to take on that cursed spirit investigation in Saitama. Nitta was supposed to do that," Gojo said.

"It's just because I'm familiar with Itadori's group."

"But that's no reason for you to force it into your schedule when you were already in charge of cleaning up after the Goodwill Event."

"I suppose you're right," Ijichi admitted. He shrugged in resignation.

"I only know about it from the reports and what Nanami has said," Gojo said. "But are you still brooding over that incident at Satozakura High?"

"T-to what exactly do you refer?"

"You weren't able to stop Yuji."

My pulse is pounding, Ijichi thought. He felt the heat drain from his flushed face, down through his spine. "Well...that, um..." He covered his mouth with one trembling hand and steadied his glasses with the other.

"I figured it out from what I heard," Gojo said. "The report detailed a messy fight against cursed spirits. Nanami didn't say anything, but he's a serious guy. He wouldn't willingly take Yuji to face nasty enemies who are too strong. As a result, Nanami came out all right, but Yuji made his own decision."

"In the end, I...um...made the same mistake as at the juvenile detention center."

"Does that mean you need to hold their hands? Your devotion is touching, but Yuji isn't as much of a child as you think—or as inexperienced. Your attitude isn't actually considerate or protective." With his right hand, Gojo cocked his middle finger behind his thumb and aimed it at Ijichi. "Yuji will be fine without all your fretting."

Then—bammo!—a painful flick to the forehead jolted Ijichi's glasses. Ijichi held his flushed forehead as the pain washed over him. That sensation pushed his tear ducts to the limit.

"*Gojooo!*" he cried out.

"Aw, a grown man shouldn't cry over one flick to the forehead," Ieiri said.

"Maybe Ijichi's a weepy drunk."

Instead of more sake, Ieiri ordered steamed matsutake mushrooms.

"I really would rather not see a man cry," she said.

"Ijichi, go home after we finish here tonight," Gojo said. "You'll be just the right amount of drunk to get a good night's sleep. Then take tomorrow off. You don't have any work, right?"

"Yes...that's right."

Tears made the sake taste different, but Ijichi finished his drink and wiped his eyes. They all tried the seafood broth, then finished their feast with chazuke with matsutake broth.

Ijichi felt good for the first time in a long while as he set off down the neon-lit nighttime streets. When he got home, he had a long and deep sleep.

Meanwhile, Gojo complained when Ieiri dragged him to yet another drinking establishment. There was no telling how long this pub crawl might last.

Returning to work after a break felt good. Ijichi's shoulders weren't stiff. His head didn't hurt. His appetite had returned. The world seemed wide open. He felt in the best of shape for the first time in he didn't know how long.

"Good morning!" His voice sounded different as he greeted his coworkers.

Asakusabashi Elegy

The air was clear, and tomorrow looked bright. In part, this was because he had enjoyed a solid rest for the first time in ages. Another big boost had come from relieving an emotional burden. Furthermore, learning that Gojo actually cared about him had worked wonders. The sorcerer might be careless, outrageous, and tough, but he was a teacher. He was a dependable person, and he recognized Ijichi's hard work. Realizing that had significantly improved Ijichi's outlook.

What Ijichi could do and what he should do were not cause for worry or regret. From now on, just as in the past, he would give his job everything he had. Having thus reaffirmed his resolve, he approached his desk in high spirits.

"Hmm?"

He didn't have a desk. Or rather, he was unable to see it beneath the mountain of documents that had grown while he was away. With trembling hands, Ijichi looked at a note on top. It was in Gojo's handwriting.

See the USB for more details.

Ijichi waded through the documents, booted up his computer, and opened the password-protected message file. A moment later, Gojo's instructions appeared.

① List occasions anyone entered or left Tokyo Jujutsu High School and all individuals who did so.

② Organize information regarding the current activities of the curse users who attacked the Kyoto Sister-School Goodwill Event.

③ Examine the details of cursed techniques using cursed tools as substrates for curtains used in the attack on the Goodwill Event.

④ Prepare methods for secret communications that are reliable and resistant to jujutsu and physical interference

⑤ Arrange for construction workers to repair Jujutsu High building and appoint supervisors from the school

⑥ Secure a budget for the abovementioned repairs

⑦ Obtain inspection permits from environmental protection groups for addressing destruction of nature by large-scale cursed techniques

⑧...

...⑨...⑩...⑪...

Ijichi looked at the computer. Then he looked at the documents. Then he looked at the computer again. He turned to the colleague next to him with a movement like that of a mechanical doll winding down.

"Um, where is Gojo?" Ijichi asked.

"He said he had business to attend to and left. Apparently, he'll be away for a few days."

"Oh, he will, will he?"

Ijichi looked out the window and up at the cloudless sky.

Oh, right, he thought. *That's the kind of guy I am. Give me a break to recover and then I'll return to work at full strength.*

He could almost sense Gojo out there somewhere beyond the blue sky. He supposed this indicated Gojo's reliance on him. With a wry laugh, Ijichi decided to dive in by straightening the documents Gojo had haphazardly dumped on his desk.

The stiffness in his shoulders had disappeared overnight, but he could already feel it returning.

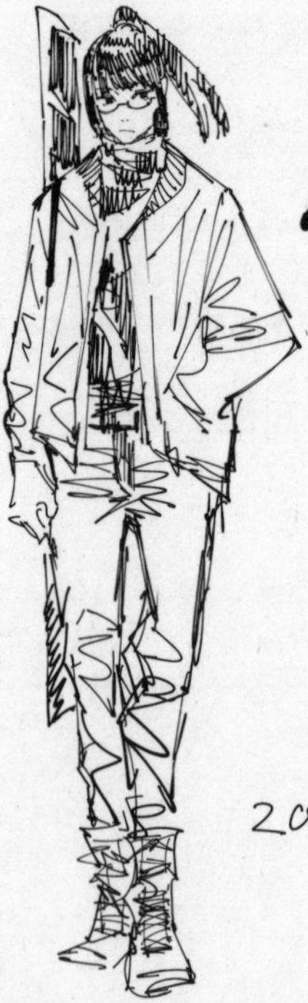

Maki
Zen'in

2019.11.30

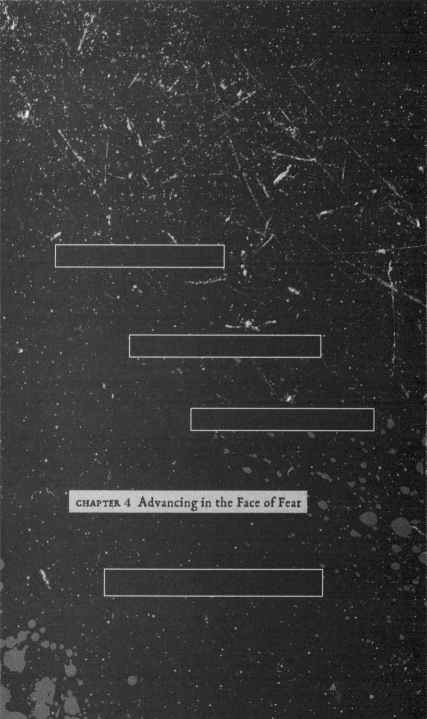

CHAPTER 4 Advancing in the Face of Fear

CHAPTER 4 Advancing in the Face of Fear

History has colors: Lifestyle, culture, climate and other facets of nature...

The town had been around a long time, so the colors had built up. Compared to Tokyo, where the new noticeably replaced the old, the old capital of Kyoto was rich in color.

Alongside the grouping of buildings referred to as "the city," remains of the old town had taken root in language, historic landmarks, and even nature. People referred to that as tradition. The older a land is, the more the colors mix, resulting in richer hues. That's why Kyoto's scenery was so beautiful.

However, Mai Zen'in knew it wasn't all beautiful. The long history of human activity had mixed good and evil, staining the land in complicated ways. Pretty colors mixed with ugly colors. Tradition and obsession, lineage and discord, sorcerers and curses—someone capable of seeing those negative aspects could never say this town was only beautiful. Thus, Mai found the colors of Kyoto, the shades that tradition created, to be annoying. That's why she was grumpy after returning from Tokyo.

"The Goodwill Event went so fast. Couldn't we have stayed in Tokyo longer?" she asked.

The girls were inside the commercial building next to the Hachi-jo exit of Kyoto Station. In the summer, they usually went to a crepe shop that sold ice cream, but now the autumn breeze was chilly, so they were sitting in the corner of a café.

Miwa used her smartphone to snap a pic of the heart drawn in the foam on top of her latte. Then she said, "It couldn't be helped. It was because of the invasion by curse users and cursed spirits."

Mai pursed her lips and ran her finger around the edge of her cup. Miwa took photos of everything, but where did she post them?

"It was too fast anyway. I wanted to have a chance to at least go shopping!" Mai said.

"Yeah, I wanted to see Marché," Nishimiya said, stirring honey into her café latte. The amber liquid adorned the foamed milk, making it look even sweeter.

Mai and Miwa were close friends, but Nishimiya was close with them too, even though she was in a different grade. In contrast to the Tokyo school, where students in the same grade hung out together, it was more common in Kyoto to see scenes like this one, with a trio of second-years spending time with a third-year.

At a normal school, the barrier between grades was fairly high. The Jujutsu Highs, however, had fewer students, and female sorcerers were rare. At the Kyoto school, where the atmosphere was more conservative, it was necessary for the girls to group up together. That was another reason these three were so close.

"Where is Marché again?" Miwa asked.

"It's in Harajuku, near Takeshita Street," Nishimiya said.

"Momo, I can see why you like Harajuku. I'm jealous of how the cute things there suit you," Mai said.

"Mai, I'm jealous of you and Kasumi. I'm older, but more sophisticated outfits look better on you two," Nishimiya said.

"Well, you can't have everything. When you're tall, you have fewer options," Mai said.

"Yeah, I hear that a lot," Nishimiya responded. "I guess you have it easiest when it comes to looking stylish, Kasumi. You get to wear suits all the time, and they look great. It's so unfair."

"I just wear them because I can't draw a sword in a skirt. And even with more options, prices in Tokyo are a bit high for me," Miwa said.

"Aw, it's not so bad, Kasumi," Nishimiya said.

"Yeah, Tokyo has cheap stuff too!" Mai said. She took a sip of her coffee, savored the bitter taste as she swallowed, and let out a quiet sigh. The black surface of her drink rippled. Then, more softly, she said, "I totally sucked at the Goodwill Event, huh?"

Nishimiya and Miwa looked startled.

"Aw, let it go, Mai," Nishimiya said. "Nobody here was that great anyway."

"At least you did more than I did, as sleeping beauty," Miwa said. "I even lost my katana."

"Yes, but still..." Mai trailed off. Resting her face in her hands, she frowned with intense displeasure. "It goes without saying that Maki fought well at the Goodwill Event. She bought time against a special grade opponent and wielded a cursed tool. Rumor has it she'll get a promotion. We'll probably get official news of it soon."

Miwa looked at Nishimiya uncomfortably, and Nishimiya looked back with a troubled expression.

Still looking down, Mai laughed self-deprecatingly. "Unlike Maki, I used my cursed technique to fight head-on and I lost. What will people say?"

"Mai..." Miwa said.

The longstanding sorcerer houses expected results. In the old houses, the patriarchal system had deep roots. It was even worse in the Big Three Families. They were hard on female sorcerers. The pressure on Mai must have been immense.

Nishimiya and Miwa often hung out with Mai, so they had a sense of what things were like for her, but no one could really know. That's why she couldn't stop her fingers from shaking, couldn't keep herself from reliving her disappointment. She was aware, however, that this had cast a cloud over their conversation.

Mai shook her head and her features brightened. "Whatever. What's past is past. Even if I had beaten Maki, it wouldn't have meant much. She's worthless."

"Nuh-uh! She should be a higher grade!" Miwa objected without thinking, but when Mai glared at her, she shut her mouth.

Urging them to cool it, Nishimiya threw her a lifeline. "Oh, well. Unlike Mai and me, you defeated *someone*. That first-year who's definitely not cute."

"Oh, the kid with brown hair who went down after a single headshot?" Mai asked.

"Yeah! She called herself Tohoku's Masahiro Tanaka," Nishimiya said.

"Even her teammates teased her," Miwa said.

"What was her name again? Obama...Kugisaka...?" Nishimiya tried.

"I don't remember. She was just a tough-talking small fry with short legs," Mai said.

"She was mouthy, not cute at all, and she plays with hammers," Nishimiya said.

"Don't be mean," Miwa said, reluctant to contribute to this kind of gossip.

The conversation broke off. Their sighs filled the air. Despite their bluster, they had all lost, and reliving it was dispiriting. The excitement of the baseball game on the second day had dispelled the gloomy atmosphere, but their frustration had remained. It was a natural byproduct of defeat.

There had been an unexpected challenge from Itadori, but interleague clashes between students weren't usually matters of life and death. Unlike the fight against the cursed spirits, the Goodwill Event fights resulted in feedback they could use to prepare for the next time. The regret in the hearts of the defeated would motivate them to grow as fighters, so frustration was an asset.

Todo would have liked that line of thought, but it felt like what was dominating their emotions at that moment was mere resentment. Just when their confused feelings were about to spill over in another round of grumbling, someone showed up who was clueless as to the gloomy atmosphere.

"Mai!" a voice shouted.

"Hm?" Hearing her name, Mai turned around.

A girl was waving at her. Her hair was dyed light red, and she was wearing a beige blazer. She had the air of a normal student stopping by on her way home from school—not at all like a student of Jujutsu High.

Looking at her face, Mai's frown eased. "Are you on your way home from school, Yuu?"

"Yeah," the girl replied. "We didn't have club today."

"Oh, right. Because it's autumn, and there's a break after all the sports competitions," Mai said. She seemed to be at ease with this girl named Yuu.

As she watched the two talk, Nishimiya cocked her head in confusion and tossed a comment Miwa's way. "Is that Mai's friend?"

"Yeah, she's—" Miwa began, but the other girl interjected.

"Sorry for not introducing myself. You're all students at Jujutsu High, right? I'm Yuu Makimura. I provide information to sorcerers around Higashiyama Ward."

"You provide... Oh! You're one of those outside helpers we call windows?" asked Nishimiya.

"Yep! That's me!" Yuu replied.

"Oh. Well, I'm Momo Nishimiya. Nice to meet you. Seems like you already know Mai and Kasumi."

"Well, she's more Mai's acquaintance than mine," Miwa said. She looked over to see Yuu puff out her chest with an air of pride.

"Yep! Mai's like my big sister!" Yuu said.

"Bwa ha!" Nishimiya barely managed to divert her face from her café latte before she guffawed. "So, Mai, did you straighten out her tie or something?"

"Gimme a break. I told her to stop calling me that, but she won't listen." Mai shrugged.

Miwa, who knew about this, jumped in to explain. "She's naturally able to see curses, and Mai helped her when cursed spirits started hanging around her. After that, she offered her assistance to Jujutsu High."

"Yep! I owe Mai my life!" Yuu said.

"So it seems," Nishimiya said. "Impressive, Mai."

Mai frowned at Nishimiya's compliment. "I just exorcised a fly head. That compliment sounds more like an insult."

"But Mai really did help me out!" Yuu said. "And I became a window so I can help her out too. If there's anything I can do, just let me know!"

"Then go get me one of those scones in the case by the cash register," Mai said.

"Okay!" Yuu replied. She bounced over toward the register.

Miwa and Nishimiya gave Mai matching incredulous looks.

"Mai, you shouldn't use her like that," Nishimiya said.

"But look! She enjoys it!" Mai said.

"You are so girly sometimes," Nishimiya said.

"What do you mean by that?!" Mai demanded.

The conversation brightened again in their corner of the café. After a little while, Mai bought everyone churros. The trio welcomed Yuu into their discussion, telling her about all sorts of things, including Jujutsu High and the Goodwill Event. Then the topic of a cursed spirit that had lately been appearing in Kyoto came up.

"And now you're tracking that wandering cursed spirit?" Mai asked, her voice low, as she sipped her lukewarm coffee.

"Yes," Yuu said. "The problem started around June, but there's no apparent connection between the locations and the people harmed. Sorcerers were unable to follow any evidence, but it seems they've learned that it's a single cursed spirit wandering around and attacking people."

"You know a lot for a window," Nishimiya said.

"Assistant Manager Tanabe told me about it," the girl replied with a giggle. "It recently caused a lot of damage in the area I'm in charge of."

"Ah." Nishimiya worried that this girl might be a little loose with information.

Aside from a talent for cursed techniques, sorcerers needed the ability to remain calm even in the midst of unusual states of affairs. Killing and dying were everyday occurrences. Even as they sat here, calmly enjoying their coffee, curses were roaming this ostensibly peaceful city, seething and cursing people. Somebody could die tomorrow, and that somebody might be one of them.

If you couldn't live with an internal understanding of that, you would, as Satoru Gojo might say, "go crazy up here." In other words, you needed to be able to switch mental gears the moment an incident arose or an attack occurred. Even if you weren't a sorcerer fighting on the front lines, you needed to stay on your guard.

Yuu didn't give the impression that she had that ability. Even Miwa, whom the sorcerers had scouted, sensed something dangerous about this girl. She cast a glance at Mai, who raised a knowing eyebrow in response.

"Yuu, you said there's been damage in your area, right?" Mai asked.

"Yep!" the girl replied.

"If you ever see that cursed spirit, be sure to inform Jujutsu High right away."

"Of course! I could never fight a cursed spirit, so I'll be sure to tell you, Mai!"

"No, not me. Tell a teacher or assistant manager."

"But I want you to expel it! So your accomplishments will earn you a promotion!"

"She's got a thing for you, Mai," Nishimiya said. She seemed exasperated, but she was smiling. From Nishimiya's point of view, anyone who understood Mai's position and wanted to help—even if that person was a little excitable—was someone to be happy about.

Mai waved her hand as if Nishimiya's gaze was bugging her. She didn't want to deal with the teasing. Just then, Yuu checked her watch and shot to her feet.

"Um, sorry, but I gotta go," she said.

"Have plans with a friend?" Mai asked.

Yuu made a point of turning and shaking her head in response to the question.

"No, it's work. The cursed spirit we were just discussing appeared at the Fushimi Inari-taisha shrine the other day, and before that it showed up near the Meishin Expressway in the evening. It appeared at twilight, and I suspect its next target will be around the Tofuku-ji temple."

"You *suspect*? Don't tell me you're investigating it by yourself," Mai said.

"That's dangerous. You should leave it to a sorcerer to chase down clues," Miwa chided, but Yuu didn't seem the least concerned.

"I know. I'm only gonna confirm the residuals. Cuz I know how scary cursed spirits can be!" She flashed a bright smile, then turned to face Mai. "But if I ever get in a pinch, come save me again, okay?"

Then she winked.

Mai's eyes narrowed in exasperation. "Okay, but only to pay you back for the scone," she said.

"Yay!"

Mai sighed and shrugged as Yuu walked off with a joyful smile on her face. It felt like a baby duckling was following her around.

"So you will rescue her?" Nishimiya asked.

"I just said that to be polite," Mai answered. Ignoring Miwa's laugh, she looked toward the café exit. Yuu dutifully continued to wave goodbye until she was out of sight.

"Mai, this is no big surprise, right? After all, you helped her out once."

Mai winced at Nishimiya's question. "Like I said, it was a fly head."

"If it was just a fly head, you could have let it go, but you chose to help her."

"Even if it was harmless, it would be unpleasant for her to witness something so creepy. To be honest, though, I regret helping her." Mai drained her coffee, which had gone cold, and glowered. "I don't like it when people get the wrong idea and act all clingy with me."

Nishimiya's and Miwa's eyes met when they noticed Mai gazing into the distance.

One week later, they found out that all communication had been lost with the window around K Girls University.

○

"It's probably too late."

Assistant Manager Tanabe was frank in his conclusion. He wasn't giving them mission orders. It was unusual and annoying to have students contact him to request information about an incident involving a cursed spirit, but the girls had asked, so he provided as much information as he could reveal.

Miwa looked at him like he was being unbelievably coldhearted, so he added that Yuu Makimura had been investigating outside the bounds permitted by her assignment. It was a broad-range wandering vengeful spirit of at least grade 2. Many cursed spirits settled in a single place, but this one, true to its name, was wandering around the city. That didn't mean, however, that it was aimless.

This cursed spirit reacted strongly to being seen. Reacting to a sighting was a common trait among cursed spirits, but it was even more pronounced in this one. Whether or not that was the case because of the personality where the curse had originated didn't matter when it came to dealing with the cursed spirit.

Some people have a strong second sight. They don't have what it takes to become sorcerers, but they do have a sense for the existence of cursed spirits. The cursed spirit in question attached to people like that, people who were aware of their own power but unable to fight back. It was how the cursed spirit picked its prey. Meanwhile, it fled from sorcerers, who had combat ability. It was crafty like that, able to rack up damage.

Yuu Makimura had zeroed in on that trait. As someone who could observe but not fight cursed spirits, she thought that maybe as a window she would be able to draw it out, and she'd made a proposal along those lines.

"Of course, I rejected it," Tanabe said. "After all, I was already being extremely careful in investigating this cursed spirit in detail, so as to avoid the unnecessary death of a window." Tanabe let out an irritated sigh. "No, I won't put together a team for a rescue mission. A grade 1 sorcerer could handle this easily, but we never have enough of those, especially not for a window who deliberately put herself at risk. Call me coldhearted if you want. Am I abandoning a child? From my point of view, you students are children, and I would never send students ranking approximately grade 3 to handle a cursed spirit about which we know very little."

His speech highlighted how careless Yuu had been. On her own initiative, she made contact with a grade 2 cursed spirit. And per her own decision, she went investigating all by herself. That really didn't leave much room for sympathy.

Miwa had that look on her face again, and Nishimiya sighed in recognition of the inevitable. Each registering their own emotions, they walked out of the office. Mai was the last to leave.

From the moment of her birth, Mai had lived in fear. Defilements, known as curses, filled the world. Mai was born with the ability to see them all, and had regretted that fact countless times.

The sky was a beautiful blue and the city was resplendent with color, but this wasn't simply a pretty place. If she hadn't been born into a sorcerer family, and if she didn't know that the world was cursed, perhaps her eyes might have registered nothing but the pretty colors.

Mai knew how horrifying it was to be able to see curses, so of course she was afraid. There was no way she could face that in a state of calm.

The memory of Yuu's voice, asking for help, rang in Mai's memory.

"Aw, give me a break!"

It had been an offhand promise, so she had no obligation to keep it. Besides, as Tanabe had said, Yuu had brought this upon herself. She wasn't so close to the girl that she had to save her. Furthermore, the cursed spirit was grade 2, whereas Mai was grade 3. The task was beyond her ability.

"So it's totally impossible!"

It was late at night. There were no sounds, but she plugged her ears and closed her eyes anyway.

The right thing to do was to let Yuu go. No one would criticize Mai for that. But it didn't feel right. All alone, Mai pondered what was eating at her.

Liar.

A familiar voice sounded in her head. A face appeared behind her eyelids—Maki's. Mai swung her arm to drive it away, but it wouldn't disappear. Maki's eyes stared at her.

"Do you have something to say, you dummy?"

With a painful heave, Mai let out a groan. Then she realized something. If she looked closely, it wasn't Maki's face after all; it was her, Mai, when she was a child.

"Liar."

This time, it was clearly audible. It was Mai herself who was muttering.

Memories swirled in her head, the scenes switching dizzily from one to another. Her older sister holding her hand. Her sister promising to never let go. Her sister becoming an adult and leaving her alone. It was Mai who was calling her sister a liar, and it was Mai who always felt like crying.

"I..."

Mai took a deep breath and struggled for words. Then she spoke.

"I'm not like you, Maki."

She holstered her pistol and flung on her coat. She couldn't think straight, so she didn't bother trying to understand what she was doing. It was probably something stupid, and it would come to no good.

Nonetheless, she kept moving. She simply couldn't bear it. Yuu believed in Mai on account of that cheap promise. Mai couldn't bear the thought of such stupidity, so she decided to go help her. She didn't want to be yet another example of someone to whom trust meant nothing and promises were for breaking.

Driven and still in a daze, she turned the doorknob. Two figures were waiting for her in the dark hall.

"Kasumi... Momo... Why?" Mai asked.

"Because we figured you'd do this," Nishimiya said, tamping her broom on the floor.

"And we couldn't let you go alone," Miwa said, resting her hand on the hilt of her katana.

"You guys are so weird," Mai said exasperatedly.

Their footfalls sounded softly as they walked down the hall. Nishimiya and Miwa walked alongside Mai as if it were only natural.

"This won't earn us any points or money," Mai said, without turning.

"I just like hanging with you two," Nishimiya said.

"Actually, money is a sticking point," Miwa said. "Let's try to do this on the cheap."

Confronting this cursed spirit wasn't worth the risk. It could all be for nothing. No one would praise them, and plenty would criticize them. Nonetheless, they kept walking.

"Hey, Mai?" Nishimiya asked. "Do you really care that much about that girl?"

"Of course not," Mai responded. "She's a twit."

"Then why're you going to help her?"

"I..." Mai tried to think of something to say, but her brain couldn't produce anything. She said the first thing that came to her, then regretted it immediately. "I just don't want to hate myself, that's all."

She bit her lip. It hurt in the cold night air.

○

There's a large cemetery south of K Women's University. Now that the girls had an idea that the cursed spirit might go in that direction, it was easy to follow its residuals. They went south from the cemetery, crossed some railroad tracks, passed a temple, and walked along a road with a rundown wooden fence dividing off an older part of town.

Empty and overgrown plots of land and moss-covered warehouses. Dark playgrounds and straggling stands of trees. This street was a veritable mass of fear, and Mai thought it would be an easy place for a curse to haunt.

They followed to where the residuals were thickest, advancing down the road and reaching what appeared to be a dead end dominated by a large building.

"This is a school, right?" Miwa asked softly.

"It was. Now it's empty," Nishimiya answered.

Sorcerers knew that large, empty institutions were prone to becoming receptacles for curses. Schools were foremost among such places, and nothing presented more ideal conditions for curses than an abandoned school in an old town.

The residual trail led inside the school. Shining the flashlights on their smartphones, the girls spotted a fresh bloodstain alongside the residuals running through the courtyard.

"Now what, Mai? It could be dangerous to just walk in the front door," Nishimiya said.

"You two stay on standby until I call you," Mai instructed.

"You're going in alone?" Miwa asked.

"You heard what Tanabe said, right?" Mai replied. "This cursed spirit is crafty. It only targets people who sense cursed spirits but can't fight them."

"But Mai, you—" Miwa began.

Before she could finish, Mai walked on. From a few steps ahead, she turned and gave the other two a mildly self-deprecating smile.

"Yeah, I'm the weakest."

Those words indicated to Nishimiya and Miwa that Mai intended to use Construction. It was a cursed technique that created something from nothing. It got good results, but it consumed a lot of cursed energy and carried a heavy physical burden. It could only be used once per day. Mai was a grade 3 sorcerer, so with her cursed energy, if she tried to use it too soon...

"It's too dangerous, Mai," Nishimiya warned.

"I knew that when I came," Mai replied. "Don't worry. After I get an idea of the school layout, I'll text it to you. Then just follow my instructions." She stepped toward the darkness of the school entrance. "Pay me back for my help at the Goodwill Event."

The other two girls watched as Mai, wrapped in a black coat, disappeared into darkness.

Curses are dreadful things. They hurt people and they take lives. They are obviously the natural enemy of human beings, who consider themselves the pinnacle of creation. Sorcerers sometimes forget this obvious fact. Perhaps that's because sorcerers have means of fighting curses, or because their senses numb in the face of circumstances so far removed from ordinary life. Either way, they may think they know this fact deep in their bones, but that is not always the case.

Even Mai, who knew she wasn't a first-rate sorcerer, had a way to fight back, and that had made her cocky. That's why she hadn't been able to think of such a tactic sooner: using cursed energy to lay a trap beforehand.

After using her cursed technique, however, she lacked the cursed energy to resist a grade 2 curse. Furthermore, she had been physically exhausted, her pulse pounding, her nose bleeding. Now she had wounds all over, like a rabbit that had been attacked. Even exorcising a fly head would be a strain.

In that state, Mai stumbled to the end of the hall on the third floor. She recalled the cursed spirit she'd confronted, and with that memory came fear.

"Fouuund...youuu..."

Its appearance was abnormal. Horrible burns covered its body and its six sinewy arms. Its face, swollen like a volleyball, featured four vertical slit-like eyes. They peered this way and that, then all simultaneously turned on Mai.

It didn't have lips, and its bare teeth gnashed as it laughed. Its expression was inhuman, yet contorted with negative human emotion. It was ugly, but long, wavy black hair gave it the faint appearance of a young woman. It wasn't human, but it had something reminiscent of human features, and that was precisely what made it so viscerally revolting.

You could tell at a glance how essentially wrong it was. This was a curse. It was an enemy of humanity that gnawed at the known world.

No, Mai thought. *No, no... I'm scared. I'm scared and I'm sick of this struggle.*

Sorcerers had the worst job. Her true feelings welled up within her. Fear, so intense it felt like it might freeze her blood, made her ears ring. She tried to make a sound, but her throat was too dry. Nonetheless, she swallowed and gritted her teeth.

Yuu was beside the cursed spirit. She was still breathing, but she wasn't unharmed. Her eyelids were bruised and swollen, and her cheeks were misshapen, as if the cursed spirit had corrupted her. Her right leg was bent and broken, so she couldn't have run. Her left arm was missing from the elbow down. Even without the cursed spirit's corruption, she would soon bleed to death.

It looked less like the cursed spirit had tried to harm her, and more like it had simply played with her until she broke. That told Mai everything she needed to know about how the cursed spirit viewed humans. To it, Yuu was a replaceable toy, and now the replacement had just shown up.

"Mai...?" Yuu said. She opened her swollen eyelids and her eyes fixed on Mai.

Mai couldn't tell if the tears in the corners of Yuu's eyes were from fear or relief. When she saw her face, however, Mai had to take bold action.

"Close your eyes. If you can't see it, it's like it isn't there," Mai said.

Mai chose the dumb option.

She had come far enough that she could no longer flee. All she could do now was proceed as if she weren't at all worried. She raised the revolver she carried and cocked it with a firm gesture.

"C'mere, ugly."

The muzzle flash lit up the darkness. The bullet was absorbed into the cursed spirit's head. It would have been one thing if Mai could have laughed about how the cursed spirit was more foolish than it looked, but that wasn't the case. The cursed spirit didn't need to dodge. Because Mai hadn't charged the pistol with any cursed energy.

"Looking... Looking? Looking...looking? Looking?"

The cursed spirit swung its long, slender arms and began walking with a sluggish gait. Its speed was like that of a snail. Then it slowly began to pick up the pace, cackling as it approached Mai.

After confirming that the cursed spirit had pulled away from Yuu, Mai was careful to hold her aim as she backed up. Just looking in its eyes was enough to make her break out in a sweat.

With a trembling thumb, she cocked the revolver and fired again. These fruitless attacks were wearing away her spirit as well as her supply of bullets. Her aim was off, so the bullet marred the wall. Then the cursed spirit finally started running after her.

Mai also took off running at full speed down the hall, but she couldn't afford to lose sight of the cursed spirit. She turned around frequently to train her eyes on it, leading it on with herself as bait.

Kicking off the old tiles and pushing off the old wallpaper, Mai flew down the dusty stairwell a few steps at a time. She looked back as she navigated a landing to see the cursed spirit using its six arms to scurry behind her like a spider.

"Those arms sure can stretch, huh?"

The arms provided mobility and had a longer reach than she had first assumed, so Mai had to be careful. She couldn't let it catch her, but she couldn't afford to lose it either. She was risking her life in a game of tag in which she could neither escape nor get caught.

"*Looking?*" it asked.

"Urgh..." Mai groaned.

The arms extended suddenly, grabbing the hem of Mai's coat. Her skin crawled, and panic drove away rational thought. She bit her lips, tried to stop her arms from shaking, and shot at her coat with the gun to blow it off.

Despite fear, panic, and exhaustion striking her over and over like a whip, she continued running at full speed. Her lungs hurt, and her legs felt as though they were in shackles. All of her body's physical signals were reprimanding her for such reckless effort.

Nonetheless, she couldn't stop. She couldn't let Yuu die, and she couldn't let herself die either. She wouldn't let herself be a sacrifice, no matter what. That wasn't just because she wanted to save her own skin, and it wasn't just because she wanted to save Yuu. If she didn't help the girl and get out of here alive, her own words would have been a lie. Mai was running because she couldn't let that happen.

"*Looking? Look? Looking? Look?*" the curse said.

"You're noisy!" Mai retorted.

Mai felt like her legs might come off, but she sped up anyway. Soon, she reached the end of the second-floor hall, which dead-ended in a plain white wall. Mai might as well have dashed down a blind alley.

"Found youuu..."

Mai turned around, and there was the cursed spirit. Its six long arms spanned the hallway, blocking any escape. There was no way she could squeeze past.

She had three shots left in the revolver, and she couldn't reload with Construction. If she forced herself to pack it with cursed energy, the burden might immobilize her, and she doubted even that would deliver a fatal wound to the cursed spirit.

All alone, one girl stood no chance of fleeing or fighting a grade 2 cursed spirit. She was like a rat in a bag. There was nowhere she could go.

"Looked. Found. Found," the cursed spirit said with a grin.

It flashed a smile with a lot of gums. Mai had once heard that the act of smiling originated with predators baring their teeth at prey. That made a lot of sense to Mai in the moment.

Even the cursed spirit could see it had Mai in checkmate. It was inching toward her in a leisurely way, as if enjoying this time, backing her into a corner and scaring her to death.

The cursed spirit's murky aura drew near. This cursed spirit would leap to kill her like a cat batting at a mouse. That was clear from the way it had abducted Yuu but left the girl alive. It would play with her, mock her, and toy with her until it eventually broke her by accident.

Mai thought of Yuu's pitiful state. That was what lay in her own future, and there was nothing she could do to change it.

Not alone anyway.

"At most, you're grade 2. Isn't that what we said? And here you are licking your lips at prey right in front of you. You really aren't first-rate material."

"Uungh?" The cursed spirit blinked, then narrowed its eyes in confusion.

Mai backed up and leaned against what appeared to be a featureless white wall. She snuck her hand into her pocket.

"You relied too much on sight."

She used her thumb to place a call with her smartphone. That was all she had to do to signal, but she also screamed.

"Momo!"

Immediately, Mai ducked her head and adopted a low stance. At that moment, what had appeared to be a pure white wall fell away, revealing a window through which a fierce wind blew.

"Uaaaaaaaaaaaaarrrrgh!"

What had fallen away was a section of false wall that Mai had created with Construction. She could only manage such a feat once a day, and she hadn't been able to create a very strong wall. However, she could hide a single window in a dark hall.

Nishimiya didn't need to visually confirm the cursed spirit. At Mai's signal, she just needed to blow wind in through the window that Mai had opened earlier. In the narrow hall, there was nowhere to run from the wind, so it struck at full force.

"Aiiiieeeeeeeeee!"

The cursed spirit extended its long arms, struggling to cling to the walls.

Mai was directly underneath the window, hunkering in the windblock it created, revolver still in hand. She loaded the remaining bullets with what little cursed energy she had left and pulled the trigger.

The gun rang out once. Under stress, her body cried out. Her head hurt so badly it felt like it might split open. She could feel blood oozing from her eye sockets, but Mai didn't shut her eyes.

She fired a second shot, then a third. The shots struck the cursed spirit. Although they were far from fatal blows, they did loosen its hands. The cursed spirit was blown to the far end of the hall. Yet even that lacked adequate force—they couldn't kill it with wind and bullets alone. Even now, Mai lacked the strength to finish it off.

But getting it down the hall was enough. Mai's desire to end this fight herself had lessened. And Miwa was waiting at the other end of the hall.

"Kasumi, the rest is on you," Mai said.

Advancing in the Face of Fear

"New Shadow Style: Simple Domain," Miwa said, opening her Simple Domain with a radius of 2.21 meters. It was a counterattack that a sorcerer could perform almost reflexively. It did not require the use of sight.

Nishimiya's wind. Mai's bullets. A corridor with no place to run. And a cursed spirit who was off balance.

Three layers, double backup.

When everything fell into place like that, there was no way the cursed spirit could get away, especially not with a cursed technique developed just for intercepting head-on attacks like New Shadow Style: Simple Domain.

"Gyarrrrrrrggghhh! Look! Look! Look! Loo—"

A single silver flash shot through the darkness and the deformed spirit split in two.

○

The next day, Yuu Makimura sat waiting for transport to Tokyo Jujutsu High. Given the aftereffects of cursed energy corroding her in body and soul, as well as the severity of her external wounds, it had been determined that Doctor Ieiri should treat her. Doctors capable of the same level of treatment in Kyoto hadn't been available.

There wasn't supposed to have been any rescue, so Yuu should have died. She had only been an external collaborator, and there was no need to reinstate her. To the contrary, she was a dangerous individual who had acted foolishly and was thus unnecessary. She wasn't a sorcerer, which made her expendable. Nonetheless, she was treated with warmth and compassion. After receiving emergency care, she waited in the infirmary at Kyoto Jujutsu High.

The window looked out on a beautiful autumn sky. Billows of clouds drifted by lazily. It was refreshing weather, in contrast to the feelings in Yuu's heart. She used one hand to open the window in hopes that contact with the outside air would make her feel better.

Immediately, a gentle breeze brushed her cheeks, and a witch drifted down on a broom.

"Hi! Seems you can walk again!" Nishimiya said.

As Yuu looked up at Nishimiya sitting sideways on her broom, she grasped the space where her arm used to be.

"They used a cursed technique to stop the bleeding, so it doesn't hurt anymore," Yuu said.

"We reclaimed the arm," Nishimiya said. "If the stitches work out, it should stick back on. A doctor who knows reverse cursed technique is going to be taking care of you, and your prognosis is good. I'm glad."

"I'm sorry for the trouble I caused."

"Yeah, that was some trouble." Nishimiya was blunt about it, but her tone of voice didn't suggest she was criticizing the girl.

Nishimiya's status as a third-year and a sorcerer was evidenced by the way she smiled exasperatedly, as one might at a small and mischievous child, and Yuu's mood brightened.

"I have a message from Mai," Nishimiya continued. "She wants you to learn from this and stop following her around. She doesn't want to see your face, so next time you get in trouble, you're on your own to die all you want."

"Mai's so sweet," Yuu said.

"You really think so, after that message?"

"Yep!"

"Okay," Nishimiya responded.

If Yuu could interpret those words in such a positive way, it must mean she really did care for Mai, even though her actions had been careless. Nishimiya understood that. She couldn't bring herself to be too hard on the girl. Yuu may have been an incompetent ally, but she was an ally nonetheless.

"Have a good life, okay?" Nishimiya said. "Otherwise, there was no point in us exorcising that curse, right?"

"Yep…"

"Aw, don't cry! If your eyes puff up any more it'll totally ruin your cute face!"

Nishimiya handed Yuu a handkerchief edged with lace, then rose high in the air. She caught the autumn breeze and flew her broom in a broad arc. A little bird that looked like it was wearing a necktie flew alongside her. Nishimiya looked at it strangely, wondering what it was doing.

Flying at the height of the leaves on trees, she lightly zipped over the tiled roofs. Upon seeing a figure standing at the entrance to the schoolhouse, Nishimiya dipped to a lower altitude.

"Yo, taxi!" a voice called out.

"Fine," Nishimiya replied. "The meter starts at 800 yen."

"A bit pricey, don't you think?"

Mai hopped onto the broom behind Nishimiya.

The broom didn't bear the double load easily, but they wouldn't have any trouble slowly cruising over to the dorm. Nishimiya upped the altitude a little despite her passenger. The sky was better for a quiet chat than the school's halls.

"Momo, your pigtails are getting in my face."

"Yeah, but I like my hair this way. Don't use them as handle-bars like before!"

"Okay, okay. Where's Kasumi?"

"She's trying to ingratiate herself with Tanabe, since he used to think highly of her."

"We should do something to make it up to her later."

Their conversation was peaceful, like gentle drops of rain. They were flying high enough that they could see far, and Mai was looking into the distance. A black car rolled up to the entrance to the school grounds and a human figure climbed inside. They couldn't see the person's face, but she walked with a firm gait.

"You really didn't want to see her face-to-face?" Nishimiya asked.

"No," Mai replied.

Nishimiya didn't pursue it any further, and Mai didn't offer any further comment.

Mai had done what she said she'd do and saved a life. No one would praise her, and it wouldn't raise her standing as a sorcerer. She had acted on her own decision and had expelled a cursed spirit without anyone asking her to.

The Zen'in clan might reprove her. They might be harder on her than ever. Nonetheless, she had been unable to ignore her desire to act. As usual, she felt like she couldn't breathe. And as usual, she was disgusted with it all. In her heart, however, she was relieved. If you take a hard look at where you are, then change your perspective, the scenery just might brighten up.

"You can really see far from up here, Momo."

"Uh-huh!"

"And the harder you try, the better the view."

"But it's hard work, isn't it?"

The world spread out before them, a wide and colorful landscape. No doubt, some of those colors were muddy, but there were also beautiful colors among them.

The world was cursed, but it also had sorcerers.

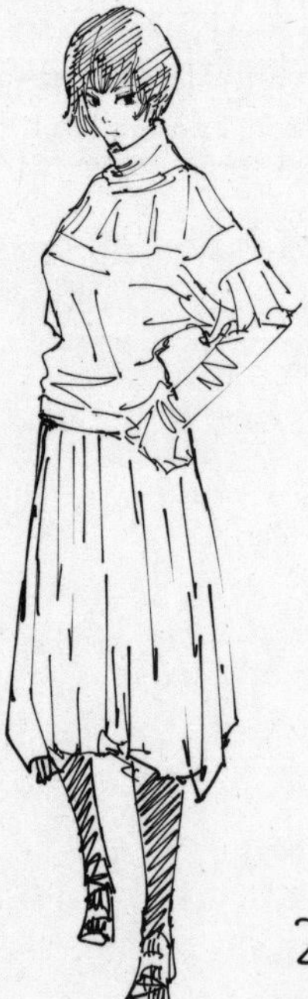

Mai
Zen'in

2019.11.30

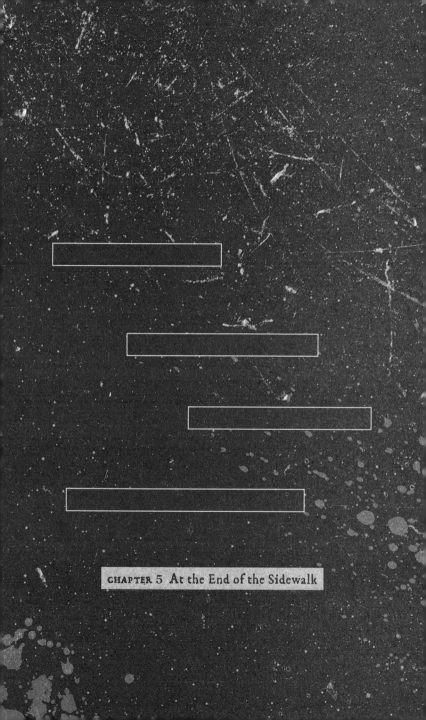

CHAPTER 5 At the End of the Sidewalk

CHAPTER 5 At the End of the Sidewalk

Autumn is the season of art and music; something in the air makes people seek out amusement. Jujutsu High students were sorcerers, but they were also students, and just as academic study alone isn't all there is to school days, training and missions are also not enough to fill a life. Students must remain ready for battle, but without a change of pace now and then, they'd fall to pieces. Their bodies and minds wouldn't be healthy and able to react to sudden threats if they didn't also find time to play. Thus, both were necessary: training to steel their nerves *and* opportunities to loosen up.

The students' nerves were on edge after the Goodwill Event, during which they had to drive away special grade cursed spirits, but the initial commotion eventually passed. Visiting students returned to Kyoto, and everyone's lives started to go back to normal. In other words, the first-years at the Tokyo school now had some time on their hands, and Kugisaki was getting bored.

"Itadori, I'm bored!" she complained.

"I can see that," Itadori replied.

"And what clued you in?"

"You're rearranging the icons on your smartphone. That's something only an insanely bored person would do."

"Itadori, what is there to do in Tokyo?" Kugisaki demanded.

"Don't talk to me like I'm Siri."

"Fushiguro! Got anything fun for me?"

"You're asking the wrong guy."

"You boys suck!"

The autumn winds were turning chill. The first-years were bored at school, and the second-years were away on missions, so they couldn't even train with the upperclassmen. In the absence of anything else to do, they walked to the convenience store. There was nothing they needed to buy, but they could check to see if any new magazines had come out, or any new soft drinks, or if the weather had gotten any colder.

Gojo had once speculated that convenience stores were a place where sorcerers, who often find themselves feeling detached from the outside world, could follow the trends. But in the students' experience, he rarely said anything seriously. Ijichi had commented that in reality Gojo probably only used convenience stores to pick up emergency donuts, but that had earned him an attack to the back of his head.

"Isn't there anywhere else to hang around? I've already seen everything in the shops around here," Kugisaki muttered as she flipped open a tourism pamphlet on display in the magazine corner.

Beside her, Itadori was flipping through a weekly manga magazine. "Yeah," he said. "Today would be a good day to go out and do something. Karaoke sounds fun, but it would probably keep us out until late, and we shouldn't stay out at night."

"And with this cold air, I'd need a proper warmup before singing Yosui," Kugisaki contributed.

"So your first choice would have to be by Yosui Inoue?"

"Of course. Obviously, I'd choose *Riverside Hotel*. Just for you guys."

"How considerate of you, but...no thank you!"

"Overreact, much? You look like you're on a variety show."

"The manga series I was following ended! Both of them!"

"Well, you were dead for a while," Kugisaki said nonchalantly, peering at the manga Itadori held. She tilted her head, puzzled at how the boys couldn't seem to avoid getting pulled into any manga with *shonen* in the title.

"Seriously? I'm in shock. Did it feel this way for Urashima Taro, from the fairy tale?" Itadori asked.

"Stop exaggerating! You were only dead for two months, right?"

"I didn't get out very often, but I guess two months is long enough for a weekly series to end. Do you follow any manga, Fushiguro?"

"No." Fushiguro didn't bother to turn away from his search for gum. He didn't seem the slightest bit interested in their conversation, but Itadori was used to that and didn't mind.

"Tch! One serialization ended right in the middle of a story arc I was totally obsessed with!" Itadori exclaimed.

"Just wait for the graphic novel to come out," Kugisaki said.

"Yeah, sure…" Itadori replied. "Speaking of which, all my manga, video games, and posters disappeared from my room. I guess because I was supposed to be dead."

"Sorry about that, but you shouldn't put up posters," Kugisaki said. "Think about how the person who had to clean out your room felt, having to see all the hobbies of a kid who died."

"Wait. You did that, Kugisaki?"

"Well…Fushiguro helped."

"Thanks, Fushiguro!"

"If I had known you were alive, I'd have kept them," Fushiguro said.

"Aw, it's okay," Itadori said.

"Why? Was there something I wasn't supposed to see?"

"No… But, well…."

Kugisaki's eyes narrowed as she noticed the odd expressions on Fushiguro's and Itadori's faces, but she decided not to inquire about it. Perhaps it was better that she didn't know. "Anyway, we can't stand here reading forever," she said.

"Isn't there anyplace you wanna go, Kugisaki?" Itadori asked.

"What about you?"

"How about a movie?"

"Is there anything interesting showing?"

"*Starshark vs. Megazombies* is at the local theater."

"A dead guy watching a zombie flick. Talk about morbid irony."

"Well, that was harsh," Itadori muttered.

Kugisaki gave him an astonished look. She was still cranky with him for not being the slightest bit apologetic about dying. She said, "I just think your taste in movies is worsening."

"Really? Over the last two months Gojo Sensei showed me a ton of movies. Some were fun and others were absolutely exhausting. I must have watched about a hundred movies."

"I bet Gojo has a bunch of weird old DVDs."

"Actually, *Starshark vs. Megazombies* isn't so bad. It was billed as a shark movie, and the sharks actually make an appearance!"

"Your geeky observations make no sense to me."

"Oh?" Itadori asked.

"If you go see that, I'm leaving," Fushiguro said.

"Huh?!" Itadori was shocked.

Kugisaki and Fushiguro seemed genuinely repulsed by Itadori's suggestion. It occurred to him that he might actually be more of a geek than he thought. That hurt a little. But he really had been packing in a ton of movies, of both superior and inferior quality.

Itadori's taste in movies had taken a nerdy turn thanks to Gojo's recommendations, but also because he had gotten along so well with Junpei Yoshinobu, another movie geek. He realized his killer impersonation of Tom Hanks in *Castaway* might not go over well in current company and decided against it. The resulting sadness was one he couldn't put into words.

If karaoke and movies were off limits, that really cut down on their options. Itadori flipped through the magazine he was holding as though it might offer ideas of something to do. But it was a manga magazine—there wouldn't be any recommendations for local sightseeing spots or famous shops. He idly turned pages as he pondered this matter.

Then his hands suddenly stopped. The magazine was open to a two-page spread in a popular sports manga.

"Hey!" he exclaimed. "Autumn is sports season, right?"

"Why? Did you just come up with another bad idea?" Kugisaki asked.

"Let's do some sports training to prep for next year's Goodwill Event!"

"Huh?" Kugisaki made a sour face at Itadori's suggestion.

Meanwhile, Fushiguro paid for his package of mint gum at the cash register. He figured the other two would probably come to a decision about what to do by the time he finished exorcising the fly head on the cashier's hair.

This was how the three first-years ended up spending a cool autumn day engaged in sporting activities.

"This is what you meant by sports training?" Kugisaki asked.

"I always wanted to give this place a try," Itadori responded.

It had only taken them around ten minutes to depart the convenience store, head to the train station, and board a train that took them to a large indoor sports center that had a few locations around the city. The offerings included a batting cage, table tennis, billiards, foosball, roller-skating, golf, and Segway rentals. And because there was also snacks and karaoke, they'd have no trouble killing time.

Sports centers like this could also be found in more rural areas, but this one was larger and provided a greater variety of amusements than most of the others. Even Kugisaki's face lit up at the sight of this wonderland.

"This was a pretty good idea, especially coming from you," she said. "Even if we get tired of the sports stuff here, we can always try something else."

"I know, right?" Itadori said. "Show us around, Fushiguro."

"I've never been here," Fushiguro said.

"No way. And you live in Tokyo?" Itadori said.

"How can you even say you're from the city?" Kugisaki demanded.

"You guys need to lose your prejudices," Fushiguro said.

"Actually, I'm impressed," Itadori said.

"Yeah," Kugisaki said. "A person needs something to do other than setting fire to oil-covered ducks."

"Why would anyone do *that*?" Fushiguro asked.

He was beginning to acclimatize to Itadori's and Kugisaki's bizarre moods. In any case, there was a lot to do here, so if he just let them go their merry way, they'd find something to occupy themselves. He was wondering what he himself would do to pass the time when he saw the arrow leading to the arcade area.

The video game corner looked substantial, but he definitely didn't want to play another irritating fighting game. The game Itadori had talked him into playing in Akihabara a while ago had been pure torture.

A huge variety of sports equipment was available to try, and Itadori and Kugisaki were both active types, so he didn't think they'd be interested in playing video games. Just then, he looked over and saw his two friends chattering away in the reception area.

"Cool! Kugisaki, we can ride a Segway!" Itadori said.

"Seriously? Tokyo is already the city of the future!" Kugisaki responded.

"Can just anybody ride a Segway?"

"Well, you don't need a license to drive a go-kart, do you?"

"Point taken."

"If we pass up this opportunity, we may never have an opportunity to ride one for the rest of our lives!"

"Yeah. Let's play *Mall Cop*!"

"What? I don't know that movie!" Kugisaki said.

"Well, at least you know it's a movie. Ooh...I like this kind of Segway. It looks like the hoverboard in *Back to the Future*!"

"Okay, you've got a problem. Is this what months of doing nothing but watching movies does to the human brain?"

"Fushiguro, which Segway do you wanna ride?" Itadori said.

"I think he should ride the normal kind. That'd look hilarious."

"Yeah, I wanna see that! Fushiguro! With perfect posture! On a Segway!"

"I know, right? That'd be awesome!"

Fushiguro realized then that they were including him in their Segway plans and stopped looking for other ways to pass the time. He might have been able to fend off one of them, but victory against both was hopeless.

○

"This thing keeps turning by itself!" Kugisaki squealed.

"Not so much pressure! Shift your weight to turn," Itadori said.

"But there is *no speed without strength*!"

"Who said that?!"

"Ayrton Senna! The Formula One driver!"

"Gimme a break! I bet he doesn't ride a Segway!"

Hmm... But riding a Segway does take some getting used to, Fushiguro thought.

Itadori bombarded Kugisaki with comments as she rode her skateboard-like Segway. Because it didn't have any handles, she found herself squatting in a way that gave her the appearance of a baby penguin. Riding a Segway was different from roller-skating or skateboarding. The fact that Itadori could do it from the start made it seem like he really was an athletic prodigy.

Fushiguro thought they should have requested an instructor, but it was too late now. He scooted along the edge of the course, keeping an eye on his two friends from a distance as they chattered volubly. If he got too close, Kugisaki might ram into him or start spouting incomprehensible comments again. He still couldn't figure out what she had meant about the oily duck.

"Those guys never calm down," he said. He did have to admit, he was impressed by their ability to keep their hyperness dial perpetually turned to MAX.

Fushiguro thought that Itadori and Kugisaki had a similar energy. He once said, "You guys sure get along well," but Kugisaki had looked offended. After that, he kept such thoughts to himself.

He had also considered the possibility that they went together well because the kanji for *ita* in Itadori meant "board" and the *kugi* in Kugisaki meant "nail." Of course, by that standard, the *fushi* in Fushiguro could mean some negative things.

In any case, Fushiguro realized he was used to seeing them like that. As he watched them clowning around, he felt like he was watching a scene from the distant past. It had actually been a while since they had spent time together. Itadori had consumed Sukuna's finger in June. Then Kugisaki came to the school in Tokyo. The time the three first-years had spent together before Itadori's death had lasted no more than two weeks, and the time they had been apart had been much, much longer. During the nearly two months that Itadori had been dead, Fushiguro and Kugisaki had felt as if something were missing.

The death of a comrade wasn't an uncommon thing for sorcerers to experience. Curses and curse users alike killed sorcerers. The number of sacrifices was countless, but that didn't mean everyone was okay with it. For those who died—Itadori excluded—that was the end. For the people around the deceased, however, the death of someone close was just the beginning. There was that first intense pain in the immediate wake of a death, and then the shock of it that dragged on like a dull ache. And if the deceased had any last wishes, they became like brambles from which the survivors could never extricate themselves.

Fushiguro and Kugisaki were no exception. Itadori's dorm room had been emptied. They had been in the habit of leaving a space for him when they walked side by side. They would start to speak to him, only to realize that he was gone. They woke up in the morning, passed the day, and then went to sleep at night, and as those unremarkable days grew, the reality crept over them that the deceased was really gone.

It was possible to try to find closure, but the past in which a friend had died—and in which, perhaps, you hadn't been able to stop it—would never change. You could train hard to be stronger than before, but the repercussions of that day that you had been unable to save someone close to you would always remain.

Nonetheless, little by little Fushiguro and Kugisaki had accepted reality, moved forward, mourned and mourned some more, and eventually left the deceased in the past. They had overcome that time. Then, as if they had suddenly awakened from a nightmare, Itadori returned. It was just like something the King of Curses, Ryomen Sukuna, would do.

When Fushiguro had confronted Sukuna, he had learned that he could use reverse cursed technique, so it wouldn't be strange for him to somehow reincarnate his vessel. But someone who was supposed to be dead was here with them. The person they thought they hadn't been able to save was here now, laughing. Of course, that was a reason to be happy.

But part of Fushiguro was at a loss. According to his system of values, Fushiguro figured that Itadori was a good person. Misfortune and death befall good people as well as bad people. Given the injustice of that, Fushiguro thought it only made sense that the world should also offer up the occasional miracle. Yet Itadori's return still didn't feel real to him. In the bottom of his heart, he still couldn't accept it.

"What's wrong, Fushiguro? Something bothering you?" Itadori asked. He rolled up on a skateboard Segway looking like an old pro. Glancing over his shoulder, Fushiguro saw Kugisaki still struggling with the controls.

"Not at all," Fushiguro answered. "Hey, how long are we going to ride these things?"

"We have to get off soon," Itadori said. "There's a time limit. What do you wanna ride next?"

"Is riding something our only choice?"

"How about the trampoline?"

"You're just choosing things that I'll look funny doing."

"How did you know?"

Itadori laughed, his face utterly devoid of worry. His personality was plain to see there. He had the smile of a good person, but it was somehow different than before. Ever since he had returned from the dead, a look of immense sadness would sometimes pass across his features. It was as though somewhere behind his smiling eyes, he was trembling with the effort of holding back tears. And his smile resembled the one he had flashed before dying.

Fushiguro could tell something had changed in the past two months. He hadn't heard all the details, but he suspected that Itadori had confronted death—his own death and the deaths of others. The deeper someone went into jujutsu, the harder it became to put on a bright smile. Since his return, Itadori had become more like a sorcerer, and Fushiguro found that to be a little sad.

"I wanna fight! Fight and win!" Kugisaki announced, jabbing her thumb in the direction of the ball games.

"Why? Are you from a warrior tribe?" Itadori asked. He couldn't help but reply jokingly to Kugisaki's demand.

"Well, you're the one who said we should train for the Goodwill Event," Kugisaki said. "So we gotta do something that involves sheer physical strength and skill!"

"Yeah, okay."

"Besides, aren't you some kind of super athlete? What club were you in at school?"

"The Occult Research Club."

"The *what* now?"

"A society for the study of paranormal phenomena. It was a comfortable group. Like us here today, there were only three members."

"Oh, sounds nice!"

I wonder how the other students are now, Itadori thought.

Not even half a year had passed since he had left his previous school. Apparently, the sorcerers had someone apply a skilled curse to the school, so Itadori believed his friend Iguchi was all right. However, he regretted leaving the Occult Research Club with only two members. That was less than the required number for a club. Besides, those two scaredy-cats who nonetheless hungered for thrills had finally learned the meaning of true fear. Did they even still like scary things anymore?

"Why're you spacing out?" Kugisaki asked. "Have you been getting enough sleep?"

"No, uh... It's nothing," Itadori answered. He shook his head as if to dispel unwelcome thoughts, and Kugisaki let the matter drop.

"Okay. If we're gonna do a competitive sport, we need something that'll make the losers sweat," Kugisaki said decisively.

"Okay, but no betting money," Itadori specified.

"Of course. Who do you think I am?!" Kugisaki knew Itadori didn't put much thought into what he said, so she wasn't actually offended. "I know! How about some kind of punishment? It wouldn't feel right among friends to make one of us treat everyone to a meal, so how about the person with the lowest score has to do an impression at the top of their voice?"

"Good idea!" said Itadori. He hadn't hesitated before accepting Kugisaki's proposal. Fushiguro frowned as the suspicion dawned on him that they planned to include him in this competition.

"I'll let one of you guys choose the event," Kugisaki said.

"That's a big responsibility for you, Fushiguro," Itadori said.

"Why are you pushing this on me?" Fushiguro said.

He didn't like games that entailed a punishment, though, so it was actually better for him to choose what they did. He looked at the guide on the wall and chose something that wouldn't involve an excessive amount of luck or depend on big differences in a particular skill.

"Batting," he suggested.

"I knew you'd pick that!" Itadori said. "After all, we just played baseball!"

"This will help us combat the Kyoto school's pitcher," Kugisaki said.

"You make a pitching machine sound like an actual pitcher," Fushiguro teased.

The choice had been easy for Fushiguro. He had at least experienced playing baseball at the Goodwill Event, so he could use what skill he had picked up to offset Itadori's ridiculous strength and endurance.

"I'll go first," Itadori said.

"No, you're last," Kugisaki said.

"Don't I get a choice in this?"

"Of course not! I'm first batter! You're like...a sports monster, so if you hit a bunch of home runs and get bonuses, we won't stand a chance! We compete for the best average in fifteen at bats!"

"Don't I get a choice, either?" Fushiguro asked.

Kugisaki ignored him as usual, picked up the bat, and stepped into the box. Judging from how she'd held the bat upright and rolled up her sleeves at the Goodwill Event, she seemed like the type who would want to run through a whole warmup ritual.

"Watch this. I'm Tohoku's Masahiro Tanaka! I'm a made-in-Japan Shohei Ohtani!" Kugisaki said.

"Shohei Otani *is* from Japan," Itadori interjected.

"Then I'm the Shohei Otani from Tohoku!"

"Yeah, he's from there too."

"Stop nitpicking!"

Ignoring Itadori's ribbing, Kugisaki focused on batting. She waved the end of the bat and tried to get a feel for the timing of the ball that was now flying her way.

"Here it comes! Right in my sweet spot!"

Crack! The bat made a satisfying sound.

The machine's first pitch had been a straight ball, and Kugisaki scored a clean hit into the net.

"You're surprisingly good at that, Kugisaki!" Itadori exclaimed.

"Of course!" Kugisaki said. "Cuz I always use a hammer to hit nails in midair! Miss the sweet spot and they'd go astray!"

"Hmm, makes sense."

There was no denying that Kugisaki had considerable kinetic control. The spare Mechamaru at the school in Kyoto had been programmed to utterly crush the Tokyo students, but a straight ball from a pitching machine at a sports center was something else.

The boys found it odd that Kugisaki compared herself to Masahiro Tanaka and Shohei Ohtani and used a pendulum swing, but all that mattered in the end was her score.

Kugisaki's performance changed at about the third pitch.

"Hunh?!" she exclaimed.

Almost as if the machine had tilted in mid-pitch, the ball underwent a sharp change—*hwip!*—practically in front of her. She continued her swing straight ahead and hit nothing but air.

"Is that thing sending me trick pitches?!" she asked.

"That was a curveball," Itadori said.

"But it curved...straight!"

"You're the one who set it to the advanced level," Fushiguro stated matter-of-factly.

"Kyoto simply refuses to fight fair and square!" she huffed.

"Don't blame this on Mechamaru," Itadori said.

"Just you watch! I stole this flamingo-style batting method from Yu Darvish—and it's pure fire!" Kugisaki boasted.

"Baseball for her is all about the big-name pitchers," Itadori said.

"And she uses a pendulum swing," Fushiguro added.

Without letting Itadori and Fushiguro's chatter distract her, Kugisaki faltered against the occasional breaking ball, but struggled on. Eventually, she began to clip them.

Itadori raised a cry of honest admiration. "Wow, Kugisaki! That pitch would've been hard even for someone on the baseball team!"

"Maybe all that training with Panda Senpai is paying off!" Fushiguro said.

"Why, does Panda throw breaking balls?" Itadori remembered Panda, who had become the baseball team's mascot.

"No, but he has a style that doesn't conform to any particular method. He teaches you to adapt."

"Oh, really?"

"While you were gone, we did so much combat training we got sick of it. Honing our physical strength, visual acuity, our thought processes."

"Oh, okay." Itadori nodded grimly, digesting those words. Meanwhile, Fushiguro refrained from adding, "But you still surpass us, Itadori."

After that, Kugisaki continued fairly well, scoring five hits in fifteen pitches. She even drove a home run into the corner.

"How about it, Itadori?" she said. "I batted 300 and got one home run. I'm an ace slugger, don't ya think?"

"I thought you said home runs don't matter," Itadori said.

"Shut up!" Kugisaki snapped. "Go! You're next, Fushiguro!"

Itadori handed a bat to Fushiguro, who entered the batter's box with an air of reluctance. Usually, Fushiguro wouldn't have taken a game like this seriously, but Kugisaki had done pretty well, and it was hard to imagine that Itadori, who had hit a home run at the Goodwill Event, would do any worse.

That meant this high-stakes game had just gotten real.

The worst-case scenario flashed through Fushiguro's mind. He would have to do an impression at the top of his voice. But an impression of whom? Fushiguro just wasn't the type to do impressions. He didn't have a repertoire, and he didn't have any ideas for improvising. If he didn't think of something, Itadori or Kugisaki would name some celebrity he resembled and force him to do an impression of that person. That would be intolerable. Fushiguro knew he couldn't refuse to do the impression. This situation truly prohibited taking such a path.

"*Argh!*" Fushiguro grunted.

Why was it so difficult?! Kugisaki was always hitting targets in the air, but even she had experienced trouble with the combination of a fast and breaking ball. The moment he started swinging, he realized his timing and trajectory were off. He caught nothing but air, and with clumsy form at that.

"You're headed for punishment," Kugisaki said.

"Don't remind me," Fushiguro replied. He gripped the bat tighter. More strength, however, wouldn't improve his results.

Baseball requires overall strength, and whether or not she was more sporty overall, Fushiguro had to admit that when it came to baseball, Kugisaki had the advantage. Given the circumstances, perhaps he should trust in luck and restrict himself to swinging straight ahead, which was easiest. Despite this idea, memories flickered through his head.

Megumi, you don't know how to bring out your best, do you?

What Gojo had said to Fushiguro a few days ago kept flashing through the back of his mind, but why was it popping up now? This was simply not the time for it, not when he was trying to focus on a high-stakes game!

Megumi, a baseball helmet looks ridiculous on you.

It was an irritating comment someone had made to him during a break at the Goodwill Event. He recalled it now because they were batting.

Megumi, what kind of balance ball would you want pitched to you on a desert island?

Now the most irrelevant memories were pestering him. In the back of his brain, Fushiguro couldn't stop summoning memories of Gojo. How could the sorcerer be such a pain in the ass when he wasn't even here?!

As these thoughts assailed Fushiguro, the white ball flying his way began to look like Gojo. He could almost hear it egging him on: *Do you really think you can get a passing grade at the batting center too?* Now that he thought about it, Fushiguro remembered when they went early on to reclaim Sukuna's finger. Fushiguro had been so angry that day that he had considered slugging Gojo.

"Fushiguro's swing is getting sharper. He's really cutting loose," Itadori said.

"And the look on his face! Is he cursing the ball?" Kugisaki marveled.

"You might beat Kugisaki," Itadori called to Fushiguro.

Kugisaki growled in frustration. "I thought the sacrifice bunt was your specialty. Have you been hiding your batting skill from us?"

"You sound like the player from the rival school in a sports manga," Itadori said.

"Who, me? Don't act like you're more mature than me."

Fushiguro forgot about different pitches and just swung for what came his way. He got better as time went on, eventually getting seven hits for fifteen at bats and surpassing Kugisaki. He felt relieved to have avoided the punishment and realized that hitting those white balls was a good stress reliever.

"Yes!" Fushiguro cheered.

"I've never seen Fushiguro do a little fist-pump before," Itadori commented. "Do you really hate competitive games that much?"

"His repertoire of impressions probably extends no further than funny animals," Kugisaki said.

"Fushiguro mimics animals?"

"All the time. Like this."

Fushiguro frowned when he saw Kugisaki using her hands to make a shadow that looked like a dog.

"Shadow puppets don't count."

"All right, I'm last," Itadori announced.

It was time for the true slugger. Itadori stood in the batter's box, adopted a stance, and used a light grip with perfect form...or perhaps not. He was too loose. Being too tight wouldn't yield better results, but the way he was standing, it looked like a ball with hardly any force behind it would travel right through the bat.

"What the hell is that?" Fushiguro asked.

Itadori flashed an indomitable smile. "You're not the only ones who've grown. I picked up a little something during the Goodwill Event."

"Oh, when Todo was brainwashing you?" Fushiguro asked.

"Don't call it that," Itadori said. "You might not be wrong, but it scares me."

Loosely holding the bat, Itadori swung, grinned confidently and christened the technique. "I call it... Swingin' Black Flash!"

Fushiguro had heard a brief account of what happened in the fight against the special grade cursed spirits, but he hadn't yet heard about Itadori consecutively generating Black Flash. *Maybe Nanami will get angry at him*, he thought.

"Yes! I'm number one!" Itadori shouted.

"How can you hit the ball when you have such awful form?" Kugisaki demanded.

Ultimately, Itadori was the champ, with twelve hits for fifteen at bats. Form and theory didn't really matter. After all, this was the guy who had been able to throw a shot put over thirty meters.

"All right, Kugisaki! It's punishment time!"

"Tch! I gotta do it, right? So I will! After all, I'm the one who suggested it!"

"Who're you gonna impersonate?"

"Watch and guess. Prepare for some mind-blowing method acting!"

"Even the punishment is like a game?"

Kugisaki flexed her shoulders and elbows, warming up. Fushiguro didn't know why warmed-up muscles were necessary for an impression, and he decided not to point out that maybe she should have tried the stretching before batting.

Kugisaki cleared her throat, struck a pose and said, "Are you nuts, Itadori?!"

"When would Ken Kobayashi ever talk to me?" Itadori asked.

"Hunh? What've you got against Ken Koba?"

"That's not my point! Anyway, why do you look so much like him?!"

Fushiguro was uncomfortable with Itadori and Kugisaki's raucous behavior. He couldn't understand why a girl would choose to do that particular impression or how Itadori had been able to guess so quickly.

"Seems I gotta show you how it's done," Itadori said.

"You're gonna do an impression too?" Kugisaki asked.

Fushiguro frowned as Itadori began stretching. This was beginning to look like an impression competition. Wasn't doing an impression supposed to be punishment for losing the batting competition? And when did it become necessary to stretch your muscles before doing an impression? Fushiguro's confusion spiraled.

Itadori made a show of taking a deep breath and then did his thing.

"You're not gonna make it."

"Enough with the movie references!" Kugisaki said.

"But you got it, right?" Itadori asked.

"If you're gonna do Schwarzenegger, why do that scene?!"

Glancing ambivalently at his two friends as they chattered away, Fushiguro strolled toward the vending machines. If they kept this up, it wouldn't be long before they tried to get *him* to do an impression.

What next? Well, Itadori thrashed Kugisaki at table tennis, then she lost three straight games of squash and got a little frustrated. They tried billiards, but no one really knew the rules. After exchanging what little they knew, they wrote it off as an incomprehensible game.

It was getting dark outside and they decided to take a break in the food court. Fushiguro was sipping iced coffee when Kugisaki came back with a boba drink. Fushiguro wondered how long those boba drinks would be trendy.

"Where's Itadori?" he asked.

"He's waiting for octopus dumplings," Kugisaki answered. She sat down diagonally across from Fushiguro. "Why the bored look?"

"No reason."

"Okay, whatever."

Kugisaki fiddled with her smartphone and Fushiguro looked down at the table. The sports center was as noisy as ever, but Fushiguro could feel the silence sitting heavy in the space between them. It wasn't like they were on bad terms or uncomfortable around each other. They had been the only two first-years at the Tokyo school for the past two months, so they had bonded to the point where silence was no burden.

But Itadori was the one who kept things lively. Fushiguro looked at Itadori, who was at the food counter with his back turned. Now that Fushiguro thought about it, Itadori was the one who had said he was "snacky." Fushiguro raised his face as if suddenly realizing something.

"Kugisaki," he said.

"Yeah?" she replied.

"Were you trying to get Itadori to tell us what he wanted to do all day?"

"Well, I said no to the shark movie."

Without denying anything, Kugisaki rested her chin in her hand and sighed faintly. "It's obvious that the idiot changed while he was away. But an idiot might as well live it up idiotically."

Kugisaki had sensed the same thing as Fushiguro. Rather than puzzle over the change in Itadori, however, she had chosen to be considerate. She gave the impression of having an aggressive personality, but in truth she was sensitive to how others felt.

"It's obvious you were at a total loss," Kugisaki said.

"Did I look that way?" Fushiguro frowned uncomfortably.

Kugisaki crooked her mouth. "He up and dies, and then suddenly comes back. So yeah, it irritated me, and I wanted to bite his head off. But I knew that stewing over it wouldn't do any good. Just like you have to accept it when somebody dies, you have to accept it when you find out somebody's alive." She jerked her chin to indicate Itadori. "He's alive and he's here. What else is there to say?"

"Well..." Fushiguro laughed then, because he knew she was right.

Itadori might be alive now, but the past in which Fushiguro had been weakened by the loss of Itadori wouldn't disappear. At the moment, however, that frustrating feeling was secondary to the reality of *this* situation, the reality that Itadori was here. There was no reason not to be happy about that fact.

"Thanks for waitin'! What were you talkin' about?" Itadori brought the smell of octopus dumpling sauce back with him.

Fushiguro and Kugisaki both looked at Itadori, who tilted his head as if puzzled.

"Is there something on my face?" he asked.

"I was just thinking you look as stupid as ever," Kugisaki said.

"Why so mean?" Itadori said.

"I'll take some of those dumplings," Kugisaki declared.

"Me too," Fushiguro said.

Fushiguro and Kugisaki banged their change on the table—*clink, clink*—and took up toothpicks. They had just exercised, and their hunger was suddenly unstoppable.

"Wait, stop!" Itadori raised his voice in alarm.

Kugisaki froze in mid-search for a dumpling with extra sauce, but Fushiguro had already placed one in his mouth.

"What's the problem?" Kugisaki asked. "You got enough toothpicks for everyone, so you knew you had to share, right?"

"These are Russian Roulette octopus dumplings," Itadori warned.

"Meaning one of them has a ton of spicy mustard inside?" Kugisaki said.

"Yup." Itadori nodded.

Kugisaki and Itadori looked at Fushiguro. He wasn't saying anything because he was pouring iced coffee down his throat at an incredible rate. Apparently, the game of Russian Roulette octopus dumplings was already over.

"Thanks, Fushiguro. Now we can eat in peace," Itadori said.

"Are you picking a fight?" Fushiguro asked.

"Sorry, Fushiguro. This was the only kind they had," Itadori said.

Fushiguro wanted to complain about Itadori buying these, of all things, but he had gobbled one down before anyone could stop him, so he had no right to grumble. Gazing at him with amusement, Kugisaki breezily popped another dumpling in her mouth.

"So now whaddaya wanna do? It's a little early for supper. Besides, we're already having octopus dumplings."

"Hmm... Good question," Itadori said.

As Fushiguro looked at Kugisaki, he swallowed some more iced coffee. He knew she wanted to do something that Itadori would enjoy, so he didn't make any suggestions.

Itadori thought as he devoured a dumpling. He smacked his lips at the taste of the sauce, cleared his throat, and answered. "We should do something that you guys want to do."

Kugisaki and Fushiguro glanced at each other, noting how Itadori had said that so casually. He looked clueless and unconcerned with details, but he wasn't totally insensitive.

Kugisaki gave a helpless shrug and laughed. "Shall we go to karaoke now?"

"Yeah! If we go now, it'll be suppertime, so maybe I can grab a bite to eat there," Itadori said.

"I can't believe you want to have karaoke food for dinner," Kugisaki said.

"It isn't very good, but it has a particular appeal," Itadori explained. "Fushiguro, let's sing a song by Yuzu! *Yu-u-u-zu!*"

"Why do we have to do a duet?!" Fushiguro said.

Their corner of the food court grew boisterous. They were no longer guarded in their conversation, and there was no longer any need for formalities. It was an easygoing, unremarkable day. Tomorrow, however, everything might be different. Tomorrow, one of them might be gone. Tomorrow, they might not be able to smile like this.

But for this moment, at least, they could sit there and enjoy their ridiculous banter. In one corner of this cursed world, the kids could enjoy their fleeting youth. They couldn't be certain that they would receive a proper send-off when their deaths came, but as they walked their treacherous path, it was nice to take the occasional detour.

Momo
Nishimiya

2019.12.1